I0743791

THE GHOST IS CLEAR

A REAPER WITCH MYSTERY

ELLE ADAMS

This book was written, produced and edited in the UK, where some spelling, grammar and word usage will vary from US English.

Copyright © 2022 Elle Adams
All rights reserved.

To be notified when Elle Adams's next book is released, sign up to her author newsletter.

Reapers didn't get holidays. Especially ones who had a ghostly twin brother following them everywhere, singing the Pokémon theme song at full volume. Okay, maybe that was just me.

Mart sang in my ear all through the flight home and continued to sing as we approached the bridge leading back to the inn. It wouldn't have been as bad if he'd had a musical bone in his body… metaphorically speaking. He'd been dead for eight years after all, and for most of that time, I'd been the only person able to see and interact with him. As a result, annoying the crap out of me was an Olympic-level sport for him.

"Please stop." I stepped onto the bridge—and straight into another ghost.

An icy sensation spread through my body, as if I'd stepped under a waterfall fully clothed. The ghost yelped and sprang away from me, looking even more startled than I was. "Ahh!"

"Sorry." Wait, why was I apologising to a ghost? They'd been a routine annoyance since I moved to the town of

Hawkwood Hollow, which was the most haunted place I'd ever been to—and trust me, for a Reaper, that was saying a lot. "Relax. I'm not going to banish you. Go about your day."

Whatever ghosts did with their time was generally of no interest to me. I didn't recognise this particular spirit, but I pointedly ignored him as I walked past, hoping he'd get the message that I had no intention of reaping his soul.

I slowed my pace when I realised Mart's singing had ceased. My brother watched the ghost, who now leant over the bridge's side, peering into the river. I might have warned the spirit of the risk of falling in if I didn't already know he was dead.

"Hello?" he called out, seemingly addressing the rippling currents below the bridge. "Are you in there?"

"Looking for someone?" asked Mart from behind him.

The ghost jumped so violently that he tumbled over the edge, which was no doubt my brother's plan. Mart cackled as the other spirit did an awkward pirouette and caught his balance upside-down in midair.

"Hey!" the ghost said indignantly. "What was that for?"

Mart grinned at him. "I thought it was funny."

"That's enough." I shook my head at my brother, whose repertoire of pranks had grown old *before* he'd shuffled off his mortal coil. "Relax. It's just my brother."

The ghost drifted back onto the bridge, looking at both of us with a petulant air. "What do you want?"

"Want?" I echoed. "Nothing. I assume Mart was interested in why you were shouting at the water, but that's your business."

I'd learned a long time ago that expecting ghosts to make any sense was like expecting a world-class debate from a seagull. That my brother had decided to scare this one was unusual behaviour—he generally directed his mischief at living people, not fellow spirits—but the ghost's twitchy behaviour triggered my suspicions.

When he didn't reply, I asked, "Why *were* you shouting at the water? Is there someone in there?"

The ghost didn't look familiar to me, but since the town of Hawkwood Hollow contained more dead people than living ones, I couldn't possibly know every single one of its ghostly inhabitants. Even a Reaper like me had her limits on how many disembodied souls she could keep track of.

"I was looking for a friend, but I don't think she's around." He turned away from the water, a mournful expression on his face. "Goodbye, Reaper."

Mart watched him float away with both eyebrows raised. "Have you ever seen a spirit startle so easily?"

"You'd be surprised." I continued onward across the bridge. "When you're dead, it can't be pleasant when a Reaper walks right through you."

On the other side of the bridge stood the Riverside Inn, which I entered through the transparent automatic doors. Mart floated into the adjoining restaurant ahead of me, causing plates and glasses to rattle on the nearby tables. Most of the customers here were happy to tolerate the inn's ghostly inhabitants, though it might have been a different story if they'd been able to hear my brother's singing.

The inside of the inn hadn't changed much in my absence, though the walls had acquired a few new posters advertising the inn's ghost tours. Behind the bar stood Jia, a short Asian woman with straight dark hair. She wore a T-shirt with a miniature cartoon reaper on it. That must be a new acquisition too—especially as the cartoon graphic bore a striking resemblance to one of Carey's drawings.

"Maura!" Jia greeted me with a smile. "You're back."

"Hey." I grabbed a stool at the bar and joined her. "The customers didn't give you too much trouble, did they?"

"Nah, no more than usual." The restaurant's quietness was typical of the lull between lunchtime and the after-school rush, when some of the kids from the academy came here to hang out. The ghost tour business had done a fair bit to raise our coolness factor in the eyes of the local youth, not that there were many other hangout options in a town as small as this one. "How'd Saturday's ghost tour go?"

"It went fine," she replied. "The other ghosts couldn't *quite* make up for Mart not being here, but they did their best."

"Yeah, I'm irreplaceable," Mart said smugly.

"Sure you are." I gave him an eye roll. "The new timetable didn't cause too many issues either?"

"Nah, I think the customers prefer this one."

"Good." After a few weeks of trial and error, we'd switched up the weekly schedule so that we had one shorter tour midweek and another, longer one at the weekend. That way, the schedule didn't interfere with Carey's homework, and we could still finish early enough on Saturdays to make time for our weekly movie night. "Which movie did you watch?"

"*My Little Pony*. Again." Jia poured me a glass of Coke and handed it to me across the bar. "Figured Mart wouldn't mind missing out on that one."

"Definitely not." Mart stole a pair of ice cubes out of my glass and began juggling them in midair. "If you'd watched *Star Wars*, we'd have had to have words."

I figured that he'd probably pick one of the Pokémon movies next time around, but at least he'd stopped singing. While he was distracted with juggling ice cubes, I leaned across the bar to talk to Jia. "You got my message?"

"Your incredibly cryptic message," she corrected. "I'm guessing you extended your trip for ghost-related reasons?"

"Demons, but pretty much the same."

Her eyes bulged. "Demons? How did you run into one of

those?"

"Bad luck." I'd thought I was going on a standard ghost-hunting trip to snag some good footage for Carey's blog, and Mart and I had gone alone because Allie had objected to Carey missing any more school.

Given that the ghost had turned out to be something else entirely, I was glad to have left her behind. Demons were among the most dangerous creatures in the magical world, and most people had no defence against them. When I relayed the experience to Jia, I tried to downplay how close my call had been, especially when Allie walked into the restaurant in the middle of my story. The middle-aged witch was the spitting image of Carey, with a few added grey hairs and the recent addition of a brand-new pin embellished with our company logo attached to her green cloak. Her matching green spectacles completed the ensemble, magnifying her wide eyes as I finished the tale of my lucky escape.

"Please don't tell Carey," Allie said. "She was already worried about you."

"I could handle it." I sipped my Coke. "Besides, I wasn't the demon's target."

Lucky for me. Demons tended to go after weak prey, and since Reapers were among the few people who were immune to possession, they generally stayed out of our way. Most of the time.

Jia and I turned to more pleasant topics of conversation as the first wave of teenagers entered the restaurant after school finished for the day. Soon enough, Carey came running in, dressed in her usual mustard-yellow uniform. Her cat, Casper, ran in ahead of her and dove underneath a table upon catching sight of Mart. The poor thing was having trouble adjusting to our new focus on ghost tours, but Carey insisted that her familiar would eventually get used to the inn's other ghostly inhabitants.

Dropping her schoolbag next to the table, she beamed up at me. "Did you have a good trip?"

"An eventful one," I said evasively. "How was your weekend? Did everyone behave?"

"Good," she said. "The ghost tour was fine. The ghosts did what Jia told them."

"I was more worried about the guests than the ghosts, to be honest," I said. "No trouble from them?"

"No, they were a pretty good crowd this time," she said. "Jia had everything under control. Nobody threw any tantrums, and no stray ghosts wandered in or anything."

"Well, the ghost that usually causes trouble is Mart, and he was with me."

Hearing his name, my brother blew at raspberry at me.

Carey smiled, guessing that he'd reacted to my comment. "Go on—tell me about your trip."

"Not much to tell." I pulled my phone out of my pocket. "I emailed you the footage, but the ghosts were pretty elusive. You know they can be camera shy."

"I wish I'd been able to give you the updated ghost goggles before then." She reached down into her schoolbag and pulled out the bright-red goggles she often wore, which were equipped with a built-in camera and microphone to pick up on any ghostly presence. In theory. The goggles were still a work in progress, given how busy she was with everything else. I certainly hadn't been that enterprising when I was a teenager.

"Don't worry about it." I joined her at the table. "You have enough on your plate."

"I guess." She turned the goggles over in her hands. "I was thinking of designing a new version that looks like a pair of regular glasses so the ghosts won't know they're being filmed."

"Not a bad idea," Jia said. "Not all spirits are as fond of being on camera as your brother is."

My brother, who'd been dancing on the table for an imaginary audience, came gliding over to us. "What?"

"We were saying that not all ghosts like attention as much as you do." In fairness, plenty of them did—they just didn't necessarily like being filmed, as I'd found out when the ghost I'd sought out on my weekend adventure had hidden under the floorboards to get away from me.

Mart snickered. "If you're referring to our shy spirit from the weekend, it was probably *your* attention she was trying to avoid."

"As opposed to the entire internet?" He was probably right, though. Too bad there was no way to disguise my Reaper abilities. "Fine. Next time, you can take Jia instead."

"Oh, no, I'm not babysitting your brother for the weekend." When Mart made a noise of indignation, she added, "It's more fun to go in a team."

"Maybe we can all go next time, then." It'd been about six weeks since we'd started running ghost tours, and Carey had started to get anxious about the lack of new content on her blog. Since I'd had itchy feet myself, I'd volunteered to go and investigate a haunted house Carey had had her eyes on. I hadn't counted on running into a demon, but that had been my own fault for taking a detour on the way home.

"I hope so," said Carey. "It'll have to wait until after Halloween. I already have people asking if I'm going to run a special event."

"Already?" *I guess time flies when you're helping a teenage blogger run ghost tours.*

"Yeah, Jia and I have started brainstorming ideas." She pulled out her laptop and set it on the table in front of her. "We had some free time at the weekend."

"Not many new guests, then?"

She loaded up her screen. "We had a group show up today, but I don't think they're here for a ghost tour."

"Why else would they be here?" Our next tour would take place tomorrow, and it wasn't as if the town had much else in the way of entertainment. Even the hiking in the local area left much to be desired—nothing but damp fields and the occasional farm.

She shrugged her narrow shoulders. "A work conference, my mum thinks."

"Weird." We didn't have much to offer in that department, as the inn had no rooms large enough to accommodate more than thirty or so guests at a time, and it wasn't near any major cities.

"What if they're here for a special ghost conference?" Mart suggested. "Maybe I should go and introduce myself."

"You can't do that if they opted out." I swivelled to Carey. "Did they?"

After we'd started running our ghost tours, we'd begun giving each new guest a form at check-in so they could choose whether to accept unsolicited visits from our ghostly residents or if they'd rather keep the hauntings to a minimum. Most ticked yes, but it prevented any customer complaints if Mart decided to prank them in the middle of the night.

"Mum told me they all opted for no hauntings," Carey said. "All five of them."

Mart pulled a face. "Now that's just rude."

"People go on holiday for reasons other than ghost tours, Mart," I said. "That doesn't mean they won't be open to persuasion to tag along on tomorrow's tour if you have a little patience."

"That's what I thought." Carey looked to her mother. "Can I ask them?"

"They've been out all day," Allie told her daughter. "If you do your homework first, you can ask them when they get back."

Carey sighed. "Right, fine. Why am I still at school again?"

Allie pursed her lips. "We've talked about this. You're fifteen, and you have an important year of schooling ahead of you."

"I've been working here since I could walk." But she obeyed her mother and reached into her schoolbag for her exercise books. The two had had the same argument a dozen times over the summer, especially now the ghost tours had proven so popular. They'd resulted in an influx of bookings at the inn, and while the fact that our name was getting out there was good news, I wished it was easier to recruit new staff to help us handle the workload.

Jia had come back to town as a favour to Allie after she'd found a certain former coven leader had left town, but unfortunately, said coven leader's departure was the reason we were having so much trouble finding new staff in the first place.

"No replies to the latest ad," Jia told me when I asked her about this. "It's getting a bit ridiculous."

Carey lifted her head from her laptop. "I can put up some flyers around at school."

"Sorry, but I'm pretty sure your classmates' parents would object if we recruited their kids to help run ghost tours," Jia said kindly. "The insurance would be a nightmare."

She made a noise of objection. "*I* work here."

"You also live here," I reminded her. "Also, do you really want your classmates working for you?"

Her shoulders slumped. "I guess not."

"It's not the ghost tours we need help with," Jia went on. "It's the rest of it. Magic can only get us so far."

"Yeah." Guilt at my impromptu trip abruptly rose inside me, and I vowed to take on twice the shifts this week to make up for it. No normal employer would have tolerated my erratic schedule—but then again, I'd never had much luck in the "normal employment" department. As a half Reaper, half witch who was a rogue in all but name, I'd had trouble fitting in anywhere before coming here. Granted, a significant part of that was more my brother's fault than mine.

Speaking of whom. Noticing my brother had gone ominously quiet, I looked for him and saw that he'd begun to entertain himself by juggling plates behind the bar.

"Put those down." I rose to my feet. "You don't want to break anything again."

"I have excellent control," he said as a plate slipped from his hands. I rushed to catch it—too late—but instead of breaking, the plate slid across the bar and landed in my lap.

"This is made of paper." I picked up the plate and turned it over before placing it back on the bar.

"I bought them last week," Carey explained. "Jia said one of the other ghosts made the suggestion after my mum said we can't afford to keep buying new crockery even if the customers find the juggling entertaining."

"Oh, good thinking." That way, the customers could watch Mart's antics without sacrificing any actual crockery. These were the things we had to worry about when working with ghosts. "Fine, go ahead, Mart."

He gave me a smug look and picked up the plate again, throwing it up in the air and catching it in time to the Pokémon theme tune.

"Not again." I pressed my hands over my ears. "If you ask me, there should be earplugs that only work on ghosts."

"That's too niche a market. Most people can't hear them, remember?" Jia joined in with Mart's singing, somehow managing to be even more out of tune than he was.

Carey laughed at us, and I smiled despite it all. It was good to be home.

Drew came to meet me at the restaurant later that evening, greeting me at the door with a kiss that made Mart wolf whistle at us. It might seem weird having a date at the place I lived and worked, but most of the restaurant's regular patrons were accustomed to Drew showing up, and we could catch up over a meal without drawing unwanted attention. The head of the police and the town's newest Reaper weren't exactly an inconspicuous pairing, but hardly anyone paid attention as we settled down at our usual table next to the window.

"You should have called me *before* you went after the demon" were the first words out of his mouth. I'd texted him the details of my hair-raising adventure, wanting to keep him in the loop, unlike the others.

"I knew you'd say that," I said, "but I also knew you'd immediately drop everything and come straight there, and that wouldn't help either of us."

He picked up his fork. "I wouldn't have left town without warning, but I'd have been ready in case you needed my help."

"Which I'd appreciate, but even your scary werewolf form can't rugby tackle a demon. They're basically ghosts."

"I know." He had a serious undertone to his voice. "You didn't put yourself in harm's way, did you?"

"No. Not intentionally." I put a chip into my mouth. "Quit looking at me like that, Drew. I wasn't the demon's target, and the person who *was* the target was in way over her head. I couldn't run off and leave her as demon bait."

I'd opted not to mention the one demon that got away without being banished, as there was very little chance of the runaway demon coming after me. I didn't need to add another column to my extensive list of enemies, and as I'd told him at least five times so far, I hadn't been the demon's priority.

Drew didn't look entirely convinced, but he dropped the subject. "The ghosts behaved without you here, did they?"

"Apparently so," I said. "Jia can handle them for the most part, and Mart was with me. How was work?"

"I've been dealing with some missing persons cases," he said. "Nothing too deadly, though only you could go on holiday and run into a demon."

"I have a knack."

"Yes, you do." He gave a fond shake of his head. His dark-brown hair had grown shaggy recently.

"You need a haircut." I reached across the table to tug on a lock, and the murmur of voices in the background momentarily drew my attention to the front door. Through the glass, I glimpsed a group of people approaching, engaged in conversation.

"I know." Drew gently pried my hand loose from his hair and clasped my fingers in his on the table. "I missed you."

My heart skittered. I wished the people outside would keep the noise down so I could pretend we were alone. "I missed you too."

The doors slid open, inviting in a gust of cold air, and a strikingly pale young man entered ahead of his four companions, his gaze sweeping the restaurant. When his attention landed on Drew and me, he stopped in his tracks. A taller man halted next to him, and they exchanged a few murmured words before crossing the room to the lobby without looking back.

Puzzled, I watched the doors close behind them. "Was it something I said?"

"Huh?" Drew let go of my hand. "What is it?"

"That guy." The newcomer's pale stillness and swift movements triggered something familiar in my memories. "I think he was a vampire."

2

Drew followed my gaze questioningly. "Who?"

"That group." I indicated the transparent doors linking the restaurant to the lobby. "I think those were the new guests. They didn't stick around, so they must not be fans of Reapers."

Vampires and Reapers didn't get along in my experience, which was admittedly limited. Drew leaned forward to peer through the doors, but the newcomers had walked out of sight. Gone back to their rooms, I assumed.

"Relax, Maura." Drew's attention returned to me. "If they're the troublemaking sort, they won't start anything in front of me."

"I never said they were trouble." Though now that he mentioned it, they hadn't looked at just me—they'd seen both of us. Even out of his uniform, Drew was recognisable as the head of the local police department, though people from outside the town wouldn't necessarily be aware of that. "Just that we don't get many vampires here. Also, they don't tend to like Reapers."

"I don't recall the last time I saw a vampire here," he said. "Are you sure that's what they were?"

"One of them. Not the others." That in itself was odd, but it was entirely possible I was being paranoid after my narrow escape over the weekend.

"We'll see if they come back." Drew didn't seem as fussed as me, but that was nothing new. He might be the head of the local police department, but werewolves weren't typically the highly strung sort, and Drew was no exception. They didn't tend to get on with vampires, but since we didn't have any resident ones in Hawkwood Hollow, Drew had had no reason to develop a grudge against them.

All the same, I kept an eye on the door while we finished our meal, but the newcomers didn't return. Afterwards, Drew and I went to the games room to play a few rounds of pool—aided by Mart, who contributed by moving the balls around whenever we weren't paying attention. As the other pool table was occupied by two of our local ghosts, Jonathan and Brian, we occasionally had to duck to avoid being hit by a floating pool cue.

It wasn't a bad way to spend the evening, but my mind kept drifting over to the new guests. Why would a vampire pick our inn as their accommodation of choice? The town wasn't exactly a hub for undead—well, not that sort of undead. Perhaps the town's overabundance of dead people didn't appeal to creatures that fed on the blood of the living. That the vampire's friends weren't fellow bloodsuckers was even stranger.

"Maura?" Drew thwacked a ball with the cue, which yanked my attention back to the present. "You look lost in thought."

"It's been a long weekend."

"I bet you're tired." He sidestepped the table and put an arm around me. "We'll get an early night."

Mart laughed. "Not planning on sleeping much, though, are you?"

I gave him a glower, hoping he'd take the hint and join the other ghosts in front of the TV at the back of the room. Brian and Jonathan had finished their game of pool and occupied one side of the sofa, while Vicky, the youngest, appeared to have fallen asleep in front of Wade and Louise. I was almost certain the pair of older ghosts had become an item in the past few weeks. How that worked for ghosts, I had no idea, but they seemed happy enough.

When the sound of loud, familiar voices drifted in from the lobby, I released Drew and peered through the small window at the top of the door. As I'd suspected, the group of newcomers, including the vampire, had come in.

"Maura?" Drew stepped up behind me.

I dropped the pool cue onto the table. "I'll be right back."

When I slipped out of the games room and closed the door quietly behind me, the newcomers' conversation petered out. While the vampire had been the first to catch my attention, the others weren't exactly typical-looking tourists. A tall man with the most striking green eyes I'd ever seen led their group, shoulder-length dark hair framing his pointed features. Next to him stood a broad-shouldered guy who was almost certainly a werewolf or shifter, with reddish-blond hair. On his other side was an athletic-looking woman whose muddy boots suggested she'd been hiking, while next to the vampire, a second woman shrank out of sight when she spotted me.

"Hey, there." I approached their group, figuring I should probably try to act more like a welcoming staff member than a creepy Reaper lurking in the corner. "Are you coming in? Or going back out again?"

Oops. I should probably have used a nicer tone. The woman at the back—petite, with curly dark hair bouncing to her shoulders—flinched, but the green-eyed man didn't look bothered by my words. "You work here, right? I'm Tam Juniper."

He held out a hand for me to shake. The formality surprised me, but I accepted. His skin was cool to the touch, but I didn't think he was a vampire. He lacked the pallor and teenage-goth vibe of his pointy-toothed companion, though he was a little *too* pretty.

"I'm Maura." I turned to the petite woman next.

She didn't offer me her hand but didn't flinch away from me either. "Farley," she said, her voice soft.

"Callum." The werewolf, who spoke in a distinct Scottish accent, also offered me a handshake. "Nice to meet you."

"I'm Perry." The athletic-looking woman then gestured to their final companion. "This is Maurice, who won't introduce himself because he's allergic to manners."

The vampire gave her a scowl, while the werewolf cleared his throat and said, "We're staying here for a couple of days."

"For the ghost tour?"

Carey had said they hadn't booked in, but I couldn't work out why else they would have come to Hawkwood Hollow. They were without a doubt the most bizarrely mismatched group of individuals I'd ever set eyes on, not least because vampires and werewolves were rarely in the same room without blowing up in an argument. They couldn't possibly be friends, so they must be work colleagues or members of an organisation of some sort.

Drew poked his head out of the games room behind me. "Is everything okay?"

Both Maurice and Farley tensed, while Tam's gaze flickered towards the door. *Huh.* Maybe it had been Drew they were avoiding after all.

"Fine." I beckoned him over. "I was just introducing myself to our new guests."

"Oh, hey." As Drew strode to my side, Maurice disappeared out the door in a blur that dispelled any doubts I might have had that he was one of the living dead.

"Maurice!" Perry tutted. "Sorry. Like I said, he's allergic to manners. I'm Perry."

She directed the last part to Drew, who nodded. "Drew."

"Tam." The taller guy extended his hand, and I wondered if I'd missed the hint of suspicion in Tam's expression when he'd first set eyes on him.

The petite witch dug her hands deep into her pockets. "Farley."

"Callum." The werewolf gave us both an apologetic look. "Sorry about our friend. We tend to turn in early… I'll see you in the morning?"

"Sure. Let me know if you're interested in our ghost tours." I usually had a whole spiel ready to use on anyone who was of two minds about signing up, but my brief holiday coupled with their odd behaviour had unravelled my rehearsed responses.

As the four remaining guests departed, I ducked back into the games room with Drew. "What's up with them?"

"What do you mean?" Drew asked. "They looked normal to me. Unless you saw something… something ghost related?"

"No, but I can't think of a good reason that two witches, a werewolf, and a vampire would be friends." At least I thought both women were witches, but I hadn't a clue what the other guy, the one with the striking green eyes, was.

"I'd say they're more likely to be work colleagues."

"That's what I thought," I said. "Or members of a club, but I can't think of any common interests they might share."

"You never know," he said. "They might be passionate about ghosts."

"They opted out of being haunted and didn't sign up to the tour."

"Or members of a hiking society?"

"Hawkwood Hollow's not exactly a five-star hiking location. No mountains or hills. Or beaches, or…" Well, anything except ghosts. *I* liked it here, but I was a Reaper with decidedly weird taste, and it was the people I'd grown to appreciate in the months I'd spent here. Both the living and dead ones.

"You're really overthinking this one." He gave me a fond smile. "There are dozens of possibilities. They might be comic book fans or…"

"Or into competitive crocheting." *What the hell? It's no less likely than some of the alternatives.*

"You never know." Drew picked up the pool cue again. "Like I said, you're overthinking it. You live in a haunted inn with a ghostly brother who's fond of hot showers, remember?"

"Really?" Mart popped up. "I had no idea."

I rolled my eyes at my brother. "Can *you* think of a reason a vampire and a werewolf would be here together?"

"Star-crossed lovers?"

"They're also with two witches and a… wizard?" I looked to Drew for help. "Know what that other guy was?"

"Not a shifter," he replied. "Does it matter?"

"You think they're up to something nefarious?" Mart asked. "Want me to spy on them?"

Normally, I'd have said "no way," but as a ghost, he could walk into the guests' rooms without anyone raising an alarm… assuming they couldn't see spirits as clearly as I could. "They said no hauntings on their forms, remember?"

"They came to the most haunted inn in the region," he said. "There's no such thing as a ghost-free experience."

"Some of them will probably be able to see you." Hawkwood Hollow was an oddity in the low number of citizens with that ability, but there was usually a one-in-three chance of the average witch or wizard being able to see spirits. The same went for vampires who'd been witches or wizards when they were alive.

Mart shrugged. "So? I can be stealthy when the occasion calls for it."

I made a sceptical noise. "You just kept the attention of everyone in the restaurant on you without anyone being able to see your face."

He flipped me off, while Drew gave me a questioning look. "What're you doing? Sending your brother after them?"

"He volunteered." Come to think of it, I'd needed a reason to convince my brother to stay out of my room that night and give Drew and me a chance for a proper reunion in peace. "Right, Mart? Want to follow them?"

"Oh, no." He folded his arms across his chest. "I'm not running errands for you without compensation."

"I'll let you choose the film we watch on our next movie night," I replied. "Twice, if you also agree not to come into my room tonight as well."

He wore a thoughtful expression. "What if I find out our new guests *are* up to no good?"

"Depends what it is," I said, "but unless they're summoning a demon on the property, you aren't to disturb us. Understand?"

"Absolutely." He grinned, gave a salute, and disappeared.

I hope I don't regret this.

———

I should have known better than to trust my brother to keep his word. I woke in the early hours of the morning when cold air tickled my ear, and I jerked my eyes open to see Mart's grinning face. I scowled at him, glancing at the Drewshaped lump next to me to make sure my brother's antics hadn't disturbed him.

"What did I tell you?" I mouthed, gesturing pointedly at the door. "Get out."

"I have news," he announced. "I know what our guests are up to."

"They're not… summoning demons?" I kept my voice to a low murmur.

"No, they aren't, but you'll want to hear this."

I suppressed a groan. The bed was warm and cosy, and I didn't want to wake Drew up for a false alarm. I gave a head shake to indicate that I wouldn't budge unless there was a demon outside the door right this instant.

"Come on," said Mart. "I thought you'd be interested to know they're monster hunters."

"They're *what?*"

Oops. I'd spoken aloud without thinking. Mart's grin widened as Drew stirred, but he didn't wake. Glaring daggers at my brother, I eased myself out of bed and slid my feet into the fluffy slippers I'd left out on the carpet. Even then, my pyjamas were thin enough that the cold air from the open window cut right through to my skin. It was still August, but summer was definitely on the way out, and autumn was keen to usher in the colder weather.

Shivering, I closed the window as quietly as possible and ducked into the bathroom. It wasn't ideal, but the last thing I needed was for the guests to find me in the corridor in my pyjamas, talking to my brother's ghost. After closing the door behind me, I turned on the tap to mask my voice.

"Monster hunters?" I whispered to Mart. "What do you mean?"

"No clue," he replied. "They were talking about 'missions,' though, and various monsters they'd dealt with."

Oh boy. The official paranormal hunters rarely recruited

from among the shifters, and I'd never heard of a vampire working for them before… That left one possible option.

"They're Wardens." They had to be—and the last Wardens I'd met had tried to arrest *me* on suspicion of summoning a demon. "Please tell me they're not local."

"No, they're not," he said. "They don't have a clue who we are."

"Then why pick our inn?"

"Don't know." He shrugged. "I had to leave when the witch spotted me."

"Which one?"

"Both."

Dammit. That meant at least two of their group could see ghosts, assuming the vampire didn't share that ability. The werewolf most likely couldn't, at least. "Do you know what kind of paranormal that guy is?"

"Which guy?"

"The one who isn't a vampire or werewolf."

"Him? I don't know, but he seems to be their leader," he said. "They all address him with more respect than they do each other, anyway."

Hmm. "What kind of mission are they on? Did they say?"

"No," he replied. "Not before they saw me."

Unease stirred inside me. "Did they mention ghosts? Or demons?"

"I didn't hear everything," he said. "I hid in the games room to listen to them talk when they came downstairs, but they left the inn, and I had to follow them outside to hear the rest of their conversation. That's when they caught on that I was behind them."

"They left the inn?" What were they doing outside at this hour in the morning? Not sightseeing, I was willing to bet. "All of them?"

"Yeah. They all had separate rooms, and I didn't hear

anything from them overnight," he replied. "Except that werewolf snores like an avalanche. Almost as much as your detective."

"Oi." I heard movement from the bedroom and figured that said detective had finally woken up. "You might have let us sleep in a little."

Mart's raucous laughter followed me as I turned off the tap and ducked out of the bathroom to greet Drew.

"What's going on?" he asked sleepily. "Is your brother trying to flood the shower again?"

"No, he wanted to tell me what he learned about our guests." I crossed the room, doing my best to resist joining him in the warm bed. If I did, I wouldn't want to get up again.

"Did he?" He rubbed his eyes with the back of his hand. "*Are* they up to something illegal?"

"No, but they're Wardens," I said. "Monster hunters, you know."

He lowered his hand, pushing himself upright. "The ones who tried to have you taken into custody?"

"Not the same ones, I don't think," I clarified. "But I don't trust them. They left the inn early this morning, and nobody voluntarily gets up at this hour unless they have a good reason."

He yawned. "Maybe they're off for a walk."

"Vampires don't get up at dawn." They did the opposite, if anything. "The witches saw Mart too."

"That's not suspicious in itself," he said. "Jia can see ghosts."

"I know." *Are the Wardens here to get rid of our ghosts? They'd better not be.* "Mart, did the witches say anything when they saw you?"

"No, they looked surprised and then stopped talking." He pouted. "They didn't even say hi."

That didn't sound like the behaviour of someone who'd come here with the intention of stopping our ghost tours. "I guess they probably aren't here to shut us down."

"No, they'd have said so right away, not checked in as guests," Drew said. "I'd say they're not likely to have come to mess with the inn. They're here for another reason."

My mind went back to the two ogres who'd come close to taking me away from my new home forever. Yes, they'd suspected me of murder at the time, but the Wardens were sticklers for the rules, and my status as a rogue Reaper put me in a precarious position. If the Wardens' propensity for gossip was anything like the Reapers', word might have spread to the other branches regardless of their promises of confidentiality. Worse, the Reaper Council had direct contact with the Wardens' offices.

"Relax, Maura," he said. "I'm sure there's a reasonable explanation."

"Yeah, but if they haven't come to arrest me or shut down our business, there's only one other reason they might be here," I said. "They're hunting a monster."

3

"You're up early this morning." Jia came to join me at the buffet table, where I'd already laid out breakfast for the guests after Drew had left to go to work. I'd figured I might as well do something useful while I was awake. None of the guests were up yet, with one obvious group of exceptions, who had yet to return from their mysterious early-morning excursion.

"I'm not the only one." When a door opened behind me, I spun around, but it was just Allie coming out of the kitchen. "I found out who our guests are."

"Oh?" Jia pinned on her employee badge. "Go on, spill it."

"They're Wardens."

Allie paused in the middle of levitating a stack of plates onto the buffet table. "The Wardens are here?"

"Not the same ones as before," I clarified. "Mart eavesdropped on their group when they left the inn at the crack of dawn, and they didn't seem to know who we were, but they're here on a mission."

The plates tipped, and Allie rescued them with a flick of

her wand. "Even so, if it's true, they're with the same people who tried to take away my best employee."

"Don't let Carey hear you say that." I didn't blame Allie for her reaction. While the Wardens had believed they were in the right when they tried to arrest me, I'd come close to losing everything.

"Hey, what about me?" Jia put on a mock-hurt expression. "Joking, joking. I know Maura's the reason our ghost-tour business is booming."

"No, Carey is," I corrected. "She's the one who set up the business in the first place, but I don't think the Wardens are here for our ghosts. They wouldn't have booked rooms at the inn if they were."

"Then why are they here?" Allie set down the stack of plates. "I wish I'd checked when they booked their rooms. I *thought* it was a little strange that they expressed no interest in any of our ghost tours, but I assumed they were friends here on holiday or work colleagues."

"There aren't all that many reasons a werewolf and vampire will willingly travel together," I said. "Let alone with two witches and whatever that Tam guy is."

"Unless they're members of some kind of club," Jia added.

"That's what Drew and I spent yesterday evening debating until Mart overheard them earlier and confirmed they're here on a mission," I explained. "They also went out for a walk at dawn, so they're not here at the moment."

"That early?" Jia raised a brow. "What kind of vampire gets up at dawn?"

"That's what I'd like to find out." I returned to putting the finishing touches on the buffet table, assisted by Jia, while we ran theories back and forth over what kind of monster the Wardens were here to find.

Mart joined in with enthusiasm. "I bet it's a troll."

"I'm pretty sure we'd have noticed a troll rampaging around the countryside," I told my brother.

"An invisible one."

"They leave massive footprints, Mart." I rolled my eyes. "What kind of creatures did they mention dealing with on their previous missions?"

"Perry said something about a possessed tree."

"A *tree?*" Jia shot me a look of bewilderment that matched my own. "Is that possible?"

"I wouldn't have said so, but the Wardens get all the weird cases that nobody else wants to deal with." Reapers primarily handled ghosts, while paranormal hunters were usually hired to deal with human-shaped problems, like rogue wizards or rampaging werewolves. Wardens got the leftovers, but possessed trees were a new one.

As we began another round of suggestions as to what kind of monster the hunters were looking for, the front doors opened, and our discussion came to an abrupt halt as our group of elusive guests walked in. Tam led the way as before, his thick coat damp and his hiking boots caked with mud. The others were dressed the same, though the vampire wore all black, as if he were making a point of playing up to stereotypes. As the thought crossed my mind, he shot me a scathing look.

Beside me, Jia eyed the trail of mud their group left behind them. "I just cleaned that floor."

"At least they didn't bring in a severed troll's head," I muttered back, though I smoothed out my expression when the group neared the buffet table.

"Has breakfast started yet?" Callum eyed the spread with appreciation, though his companions looked tense enough that I wondered if they'd picked up on the general mood. The petite witch's hands were clenched so tightly that her knuckles were white.

"It starts at seven," Allie replied with more frost in her tone than I'd ever heard her display towards a guest before. That didn't go unnoticed by the others, and the white-knuckled witch moved towards the door as if to leave.

"You can wait in here until then," added Jia, without quite managing to conjure up her usual friendly customer-service tone. "We actually have a few questions we wanted to ask you."

I gave her a warning look, but her face was set. *She wants to confront them now?* I guessed it was wiser to get it out of the way before the other guests showed up, but that didn't mean I looked forward to the idea of potentially burning bridges.

Allie blew out a breath. "Carey will be down in a minute. I'll see where she is."

Translation: she wanted to make sure Carey didn't come in when we were in the middle of a confrontation. Not that I *wanted* an argument, but my track record spoke for itself. The rest of us watched her leave, waiting for someone to break the fraught silence.

The vampire spoke for the first time, in a soft Yorkshire accent. "Is there a problem?"

"Depends if you're here to report us or not." Jia gave him a hard stare. "To the Wardens."

Tam's shoulders stiffened, but his expression showed more confusion than anything else. "Report you? Why would we do that?"

"We had a run-in with another group of your people not long ago," Jia told him. "It wasn't the most pleasant encounter."

"They threatened to shut down our business." I decided to skip over the part where they'd nearly arrested me as a rogue Reaper. "I know your people deal with ghosts sometimes..."

"Ghosts?" said the athletic woman, Perry. "Nah, they're

too tame for us. You have a haunted house thing going here, don't you? We won't interfere with that. Don't worry."

"Then why are you here?" I scanned their group, wondering who'd thought it was a good idea to put a vampire and a werewolf together in the same group. That seemed a recipe for disaster if I ever saw one, and that wasn't counting the witches either. "Hunting a monster?"

"Our mission is classified," Tam said, his tone polite but firm. "We're under orders not to disclose the details, but rest assured we pose no threat to your business or to the employees of your inn."

"Unless they keep following us around," the vampire said in a carrying whisper.

Oh boy. He can definitely see my brother.

"You're staying at a haunted inn," I informed him. "Expecting it to be free of ghosts is like staying on a hotel next to a beach and complaining about the seaside view."

"That's right." Mart drifted over, sticking his tongue out at the vampire. "We were here before you."

Maurice gave a soft snort. "We opted out of your party tricks on those forms when we checked in."

"You opted out of us coming into your rooms," Mart corrected. "You didn't opt out of us haunting you everywhere else."

Tam and Callum both looked confused enough that it was clear *they* couldn't see ghosts, but three out of five was enough to pose a problem.

"Whatever the reason you're here, all of our guests get a discount on our ghost tours." Jia switched back to her friendly customer-service tone. "The next one's this evening, and we have a few spaces if any of you are interested."

The athletic-looking witch was the only one of their group who looked mildly intrigued, but Maurice gave a firm shake of his head. "Not interested. Tell you what—we should find somewhere else to stay. What do you guys think?"

Callum moved to the vampire's side. "Drop it, Maurice. You're being unnecessarily rude."

"There isn't anywhere else to stay in the area," Perry added. "If I'd nearly had my business shut down by the Wardens, I'd be suspicious too."

"Why would the Wardens shut you down?" Maurice swivelled back to Jia and me. "Got something to hide?"

Dammit. I'd walked into that one, and I wished I'd come up with a plausible cover story that didn't expose my Reaper status to a group of Wardens.

"Maybe we're hiding bodies in the basement," Mart said. "Want to join them?"

"Mart, that's enough." I gave him a warning look. "Everyone simmer down. You're welcome to leave the inn or stay, but you can't opt out of seeing the ghosts. They're residents here too."

"That's right," Mart said. "And you're the ones with something to hide. Looking for a bogeyman, are you?"

Tam beckoned the vampire over and murmured something into his ear. Maurice scowled, replying in a carrying whisper, "They want to know our mission. Are you sure you want ghosts following us around, asking nosy questions?"

Tam stepped away from the vampire and addressed Jia and me. "I'm not joking when I say we could get into a lot of trouble if the head office finds out we've shared any details of our mission outside of our group. We came here because we needed accommodation in the area, for no other reason. Nothing we do will affect you."

That remained to be seen, but I didn't particularly *want* to kick out our guests and earn the enmity of another group of Wardens for no good reason. Besides, if there *was* a monster in the area, I'd rather leave it to a group of monster hunters than have to deal with it myself.

"All right," I said. "Keep your secrets, but if we see any signs that you're doing anything that might endanger the employees of the inn or our guests, we have the right to kick you out. Deal?"

"Sounds fair," said Perry. "Right, Tam?"

He nodded—reluctantly, I thought—while the petite woman's hands slowly unclenched.

"That sounds fair." The werewolf's attention turned back to the table. "Can we help ourselves to breakfast now?"

"Go right ahead." I stepped aside and surreptitiously pulled out my wand to clean up the trail of mud they'd left behind them.

Mart remained by the table, juggling plates, until Maurice glided out of the lobby with the speed only vampires possessed. I caught my brother's eye, and he zipped after the vampire, dropping the plates all over the floor as he did so. Doubly glad that Jia had had the forethought to replace them with paper ones, I went to pick up the plates and hoped that Mart would make more of an effort to stay out of the vampire's line of sight this time.

By the time the rest of the Wardens had filled their plates, more of the guests had begun to file into the restaurant.

"I'll keep an eye on them," Jia murmured, watching the group of four pick out a table near the window. "Even if they aren't here to shut us down, who's to say whatever monster they're hunting won't show up here next?"

"If they're good at their jobs, they ought to deal with this monster without us having to do anything ourselves."

"I hope you're right." She waved at Carey, who'd just entered with her mother. "Hey, Carey. Ready for school?"

"Not really," said Carey. "I'd rather be planning tonight's tour."

"You need to focus on your schoolwork." Allie had pushed her daughter into taking a summer school programme over the holidays, saying it was good for her to get out of the inn, but Carey's education had been a point of contention between the pair of them for the past few weeks.

Carey sighed. "I know."

"You can take the opportunity to advertise the tours to your classmates too." I tended to stay out of their arguments, but personally, I wasn't one to stand in favour of traditional magical education. I'd done nothing with my own, after all. "Did you already take our entire stash of flyers with you to school?"

She gave a sheepish grin. "My teacher kept taking them down. She said I went overboard."

"Hey, it's marketing." I crouched down to pet Casper the cat when he padded over to join her at the table. "And it gives your familiar a break from the ghosts."

"Yeah." She let Casper climb into her lap, while her mother returned with a plate for her and a saucer of milk for her familiar. "He seems to be more tolerant of them than he used to be."

"Good." How she'd ended up with a familiar who was terrified of ghosts was a mystery to me, given her ghost-hunting hobby had gone on for far longer than her ambitions to turn the inn into a haunted hot spot. Poor Casper had spent the first two weeks of our ghost tours hiding underneath Carey's bed.

Jia and I chatted to Carey and Allie while we kept an eye on the Wardens' table, but the new guests remained huddled in a group, talking in low voices and otherwise not drawing attention to themselves. I walked past their table a couple of times on the pretext of clearing away their plates, but the clamour of noise from the other guests made it hard to make out any of their conversation. If I'd had to guess, Tam had told the others not to discuss official Warden business while inside the inn, so I didn't make an overt effort to approach them until after Carey had left for school.

"You're staying in?" I walked past their table, carrying a stack of plates. "Or do you want recommendations of things to do in the area?"

"No, we're good," Callum said around a yawn. "We'll go out later. I might take a nap."

"You were up early," I observed. "Do you normally go out at dawn?"

I'd hoped to get a clue about what they were looking for —most monsters were typically active at night—but they didn't take the bait.

"Me?" Callum asked. "No, but Perry and Tam are."

"Weirdos," added Farley, who seemed to have relaxed considerably since the vampire's departure had signalled an end to our clash earlier. "I'll have a nap too."

"All right, but set an alarm," Tam told her. "Set one for Maurice too. I bet he's forgotten."

Perry made a sceptical noise. "If he thinks there's a ghost watching him, he's probably still awake."

If not for the vampire's obvious attitude problem, I might have felt bad for him having to put up with Mart following him around, but if anyone deserved to put up with my brother's singing, it was Maurice.

Their group departed the restaurant, leaving me at something of a loose end. I texted Drew, summing up what Jia and I had learned about the newcomers, and then got on with my shift. Jia and I fell into our usual routine as customers began to show up at the restaurant for a late breakfast while guests dropped by with compliments and questions about the ghost tour.

I'd almost managed to forget our strange new guests—at

least until Drew finally replied to my message later that morning with an ominous one-line text. *Don't leave the inn.*

"Don't leave the—" *He has to be kidding, right?* I peered through the window across from the bar, but rain blurred the glass, making it impossible to see what he wanted me to avoid. I messaged back: *What???*

We found a body in the river.

The phone slipped from my fingers, clattering onto the bar.

"What is it?" asked Jia.

"Drew said the police found a body." I scooped up my phone, holding it gingerly in both hands. "In the river."

Her eyes grew round. "*Where* in the river?"

"He said, 'Don't leave the inn,' so it must be close." I looked for my brother, but he hadn't returned from following the vampire. From this angle, we could see a small section of the river through the windows, but I didn't see any police outside.

"Was it one of those missing people he was talking about?" Jia strode around the bar. "I'll have a look."

She crossed the restaurant to the front, and the automatic doors slid open. I grimaced, though technically, Drew hadn't told *her* not to leave the inn. After a pause, she stepped back from the doors and returned to the bar. "There's nobody out there."

"Then why…?" My blood chilled. "Am I paranoid for thinking this might be connected to our mysterious visitors?"

"No, but if we're looking at another serial killer or just a one-off murder, that's not the Wardens' business."

And if not? I knew better than to ignore a coincidence when I saw one. If there was any trouble in town, chances were high that it had arrived alongside our new guests.

4

Drew didn't show up until lunchtime, by which time I'd worn a hole in my shoes from pacing up and down behind the bar. Jia was in a similar state, and I'd had to talk her out of going upstairs to eavesdrop on our guests in their rooms.

"They're just sleeping, Jia," I told her. "I can guarantee they have an unspoken agreement not to discuss anything related to their mission inside the building, in case anyone is listening. Incorporeal or otherwise."

"Mart's still upstairs," she observed. "Why hasn't he come back?"

"You know him. He gets distracted easily." If the vampire was up to anything dodgy, Mart wouldn't have let him get away without warning me, so I returned my attention to work—and pacing.

When the front doors opened, I lifted my head, expecting to see Drew. Instead, my brother came drifting in, showering the floor in raindrops, and proceeded to make a big show of shaking nonexistent water out of his hair.

"Where have you been?" I asked. "I didn't know you went outside."

"I thought you wanted me to follow our delightful guest."

"That sneaky vampire." I'd assumed he'd gone back to his room, but he must have changed directions on the way. "Where is he?"

"Wandering around the countryside," replied Mart. "I got bored watching him hunting rats—which is disgusting and uncivilised, by the way. I told him not to bring them back to the inn."

"Lovely." I gave a shudder. "Did you see Drew on the way back? He said they found a body in the river."

"Ooh, whose?"

"Possibly one of their missing persons." I looked up sharply when Drew entered the restaurant. "There he is."

Drew reached the bar and ran a hand through his damp hair. "Hey, Maura. Sorry for the cryptic messages."

"I hope you have a good reason for freaking me out," I said. "Did the body you found belong to one of your missing persons?"

He inclined his head. "Yes. A young witch who disappeared yesterday morning."

"How… How did she die?"

He wore an uneasy expression. "It seems that she drowned, but we haven't had time to examine the body."

My mind flickered back to the ghost I'd seen peering into the river over the bridge. He'd been looking for someone… Might it have been the missing witch? "If her death was an accident, why would you warn me not to leave the inn?"

"Because I know what you're like, Maura."

"Oi." *Come on.* I didn't *always* show up at murder sites— just a little more frequently than the average person. "I saw a ghost yesterday on the bridge. He was calling to someone in the water. Might there be a connection?"

His brows shot up. "Don't ask me. You're the expert on ghosts."

"Yeah, but ghosts are weird." I dropped my voice as the door to the lobby slid open and a certain group of guests walked in… with one obvious vampire-shaped exception.

Drew followed my gaze, furrowing his brow, but he didn't move to speak to the newcomers. Neither did I, though I watched out of the corner of my eye as they sat at the same table they had earlier. Evidently, they'd decided to stay at the inn for lunch. Given the rain sheeting down outside, I didn't blame them for staying put.

"I'll take their order." Jia strode across to their table, while I angled myself that way so I could hear her talking to them. "Hey, there. Want to try one of our lunchtime specials?"

While our menus were enchanted so that customers could order by tapping on their choice without anyone having to talk to them, I figured Jia wanted to introduce the specials in person in order to have an excuse to ask a few more questions.

Drew leaned over to watch the Wardens too. "There's only four of them. One is missing."

"The vampire," I said. "Mart followed him around the countryside for a bit, but he got bored."

"Was the vampire aware he was being followed?"

"Oh, he was," I said. "He can see ghosts, and he was downright rude to us earlier. I figured he deserved to listen to Mart's out-of-tune singing for hours."

"Hey, I sing like an angel," my brother protested, overhearing. "I've been practising a new ballad to demonstrate at the ghost tour tonight."

"Please don't." I gave a surreptitious glance at our guests, but Perry and Farley were too busy politely refusing Jia's offer of a Halloween All Year Round Special to notice Mart, and the other two couldn't see or hear him. "Drew, I know you can't stay long, but I wondered… Do you think there might have been, ah, something other than a human involved in the witch's death?"

He shook his head. "I honestly couldn't say, but I have a hard time believing a witch could have drowned without trying to save herself. She was holding her wand when we fished her out of the river too."

"Weird." *Or not if she'd been taken by surprise.* Those river currents were unpredictable, and even a witch could succumb to cold or shock. "Whereabouts did you find her?"

"Just outside the town's boundaries, but it's possible the river's current carried her downstream."

"Hmm." I lifted my gaze to the newcomers, who'd gone quieter. I hoped they weren't listening in.

"Your friend isn't joining you?" Jia asked Tam, presumably referring to Maurice.

"He prefers to eat alone," said Perry, distaste layering her voice.

"I suppose he can't bring his victims to the dinner table without ruining everyone else's appetites." Mart, seeing a new target, drifted over to their table.

"He doesn't feed on humans," said Farley, a surprisingly defensive note to her voice.

"Really?" Jia asked. "Weird. Is that some kind of Warden rule?"

"No, it's a personal choice," said Tam. "We have to live together, and it's better that we all get along."

"You live together?" I walked across to join them, giving up on pretending not to listen. "In a house?"

"A castle, actually," said Perry.

"An actual castle?" That, I hadn't expected. "Seriously?"

"More of a tower," she clarified. "But it's been updated to make it livable for modern humans, so there's central heating and everything, but it's a real medieval castle."

"Good," said Mart. "I wouldn't want to stay anywhere without a shower."

Perry frowned at him. "You're a ghost. You can't feel—"

"Don't finish that sentence," I warned. "He's a little sensitive."

"Are you siblings, by any chance?" Farley looked between us. "You are, right?"

"Who are you talking to?" Callum asked in confusion. "Whose sibling?"

"My brother, Mart," I said to the table at large, gesturing at Mart's hovering figure. "He works for the inn. We have five other ghost employees too."

Tam blinked in apparent surprise. "And… your guests can't see them?"

"No, but our staff can." I opted not to mention that Carey and Allie didn't share that ability, since it was up to them whether they wanted the guests to know or not. "Like I said, we still have tickets for the evening's tour available if you want to see them in action, but I guess that depends if you're busy with something else."

The others must have heard "something else" as "monster hunting." To be fair, that was exactly what I meant. Farley's interested expression vanished, Callum's gaze turned downward, and Tam's shoulders tensed. Perry, meanwhile, waved to Drew, who'd joined us.

"I can vouch for the ghost tours," he said, "but I won't be there. Sorry, Maura. I have to get back to work."

"No worries." I walked with him to the door, gave him a brief kiss goodbye, and then returned to the Wardens' table.

"He's your boyfriend?" Perry guessed.

"Yeah, Drew's the head of the local police force." I studied their faces to see how they reacted, but only Farley gave a visible response, her hands gripping her seat. "He's busy working on an investigation. There've been a few disappearances in town recently."

Jia's brows shot up, but the others' reaction told me I'd made the right call by mentioning Drew's investigation aloud. Perry's mouth dropped open, Farley bolted to her feet, and Callum blurted, "Disappearances?"

Tam, the only person who hadn't reacted, cleared his throat.

The werewolf blushed, but it was too late to hide his response. "Ah—who disappeared?"

"Police business," I said blithely. "Unless, that is, it's linked to this mission of yours. I gather the Wardens sometimes work with the local authorities?"

"Sometimes," Perry said, a thoughtful note to her tone. "Right, Tam?"

"If that's the case," I went on, "you might be able to get permission to work with Drew's team… but only if you share what *you* know."

Tam rose to his feet, seemingly forgetting about ordering anything to eat. "In that case, we'll pay them a visit."

"Not now," said Perry. "We just sat down. Can't we go after lunch?"

"Not sure I want to look at a dead body after eating," remarked Callum.

"I doubt you'll get to look at the body," I told them. "Even if you convince Drew to let you in, there are rules. I should know."

"You don't work for the police." Tam studied my face. "Or do you?"

"No, but I do work with ghosts, and they tend to show up after someone dies." There was also the one on the bridge I wanted to flag down, but not with the Wardens present.

"Come on." Callum gestured to Tam, who sat back down. "We'll order and decide what to do afterwards."

I was on board with that plan, because a queue had begun to form at the bar, signalling that the lunchtime rush was about to start. Jia and I soon had our hands full dealing with customers. We didn't even have time to grab anything to eat ourselves, which was probably my fault for getting distracted by our guests. Typically, the Wardens spent the bare minimum of time on their meals before getting up to leave.

I hastened to waylay them at the door. "Wait. You don't know the way to the police station, do you?"

"Sure, we walked past it on the way here," said Callum.

"But you don't know anyone there except for Drew."

"We can talk our way in. It's fine," Perry replied.

"Uh-huh." I looked to her leader, who did admittedly look like the sort of person who could talk his way into a high-class hotel or a dingy nightclub in equal measures. "Are you sure you want to gamble your mission on that?"

Jia grabbed my arm and pulled me aside, whispering, "Hey, Maura! I'll cover for you here. I know you want to go with them."

Guilt squirmed inside me. "I just got back. I can't leave you to handle everything alone."

"Allie will help me out," she said. "I know you want to stay in the loop on this, and didn't you have a ghost you wanted to talk to?"

"Not in front of witnesses." That would have to wait until later. "I'll try to be quick. If the police shut the door in their faces, I'll come straight back here."

"Drew wouldn't do that, would he?"

"No, but some of his officers aren't known for being friendly to outsiders."

While the Wardens probably had some official paperwork or permission from their head office, whether they would be allowed to get involved depended on whether the police believed their mission was in any way linked to the ongoing missing persons investigation. Given my track record, it could go either way, though contrary to what certain officers believed, I only got involved in police investigations when I had no choice in the matter. Or when people tried to have me arrested.

I went into the lobby to explain to Allie where I was going and then jogged out of the inn to catch up to the Wardens. They'd pulled their hoods up against the rain and stood in a huddle on the other side of the bridge, waiting for… *Not me, surely.* Then I saw the vampire approaching from the other direction. *Oh, him.*

Maurice gave me an ugly look. "What's she doing here?"

"Helping you get in to talk to the police."

"We don't need help," said the vampire. "Tam, you didn't tell *her* about the mission, did you?"

"He didn't need to." I hitched on a smile. "I assume your mission is connected to the police's current open investigation into several disappearances, on which my boyfriend is the lead investigator. So, shall we be off?"

Perry laughed under her breath at the expression on the vampire's face. "She's got you there, Maurice."

"Drop it," Tam told them both as the vampire opened his mouth to display some impressively sharp teeth. "I want you all on your best behaviour. Got that?"

How long had they all been working together? Less time than I'd initially guessed, judging by the way the vampire was obviously ill at ease with Perry in particular. Unless it was just my presence that grated on him. My brother's too. Mart hadn't followed me outside, and I didn't need him causing any distractions while we talked to the police, so I decided to leave him with Jia.

While Hawkwood Hollow was small enough that it wouldn't have been hard for the Wardens to find the police station on their own, Tam let me walk in front of their group and lead the way to the small brick building that served as the town's only police department.

Inside the lobby, Drew paused when he saw us enter through the automatic doors. "Maura? I thought you were at work."

"The Wardens would like to talk to you." *Might as well get it out in the open.* "About the investigation."

"Really?" He eyed Tam, who inclined his head.

"Yes, if you're willing to speak to us," Tam said. "We have a permit."

"Then you'd better come in." Drew beckoned us into a small room that served as his office, while everyone in the lobby looked on in confusion—or disapproval, in the case of Petra, an officer who had a particular dislike of me. Before she could raise an objection, Drew ushered us into the room and closed the door.

"Right," said Drew, positioning himself behind the desk while the rest of us crammed ourselves into the remaining space. "Where's this permit of yours?"

"Here." Tam slid his hand into his pocket and produced a slim file. "We can work with the local authorities on any mission… Why is she staying in here?" He indicated me, and I bristled when everyone looked at me.

"Because I can see ghosts, of course," I said. "Next question?"

"Maura stays," said Drew over the vampire's audible scoff. "I can't say we've had pleasant experiences with your people recently."

"I heard," said Tam, "but we're not local. We're based in Northumberland."

"You came a long way." He took the file, flipping it open, and scanned the document inside.

"Our missions take us all over the country," said Tam.

"Maura said you were investigating disappearances. When did they start?"

"Last week," Drew replied. "Your paperwork doesn't state the details of your mission."

"That's because we don't know," Perry said. "We figure it's a monster, because that's what the reports said, but the official order said we're just here to check for any trouble."

"What reports?" Drew closed the file and handed it back to Tam. "Who exactly gave you the mission?"

"The Wardens' head office is responsible for assigning missions to each team," said Tam. "As team leader, I have some freedom to choose our missions, so I picked this one because it seemed to suit our strengths."

What strengths? I suppressed the urge to ask the question aloud; the five of them might be a mismatched team, but a vampire was a nasty opponent in a fight, and werewolves were no pushovers either.

"Someone from here must have contacted the head office in the first place." Drew sounded displeased. "I'll look into that, but in the meantime, I'm afraid we don't have any use for your... ah, skills. There's no proof that woman's death was anything other than an accident, and if not, the perpetrator was most likely human."

"Your eyes don't see everything," said Maurice.

With spectacular timing, Mart materialised into the already-cramped office. Not that he took up much space as a ghost, but upon seeing him, Farley backed towards the door.

"It's too stuffy in here," she said. "I'm going to wait outside."

"Me too," said Callum.

Mart put on a hurt expression. "That's nice."

"It *is* stuffy in here." I didn't budge, though. "Besides, you're supposed to be at the inn, Mart."

"You left me behind!"

"Don't you have a ghost tour to prepare for?" I turned my attention back to Drew and Tam, neither of whom had seen the intruder, though of course they'd heard my side of the conversation. "Back to the subject at hand—what's the plan?"

"I'm not supposed to let this many people in on an official investigation." Drew had a mildly guilty undertone to his voice. "Like I said, there's no proof of paranormal involvement, and the body is in the morgue, waiting for examination."

"That wasn't an invitation," I told Maurice, who'd moved imperceptibly towards the door. "You aren't allowed to wander into the morgue."

"Then we can't do our jobs, can we?" The vampire shook his head. "C'mon, Tam. We'll do this alone."

"That doesn't mean I'm not open to cooperation," Drew added. "I'll talk to my staff and see what I can do, but like I said, unless more evidence emerges…"

"What about the other disappearances?" asked Tam. "How many were there?"

"Three," he replied. "Nothing to link them except they vanished within the last few days."

"That sounds like enough of a connection," said Tam. "Were they all in a similar location when they vanished? Did they have anything else in common?"

"The first part, we don't know, since there were no witnesses," he replied. "Two were wizards, two witches, including the one whose body we found. We're still looking to see if they were acquainted beforehand."

"Weird," I said. "Are the police searching the river for the others too?"

"They are, but so far, none of them have shown up," Drew said. "Our next step is to talk to people who saw the victims before they vanished, but I'm afraid that isn't something I can bring outsiders into."

"That's fine," said Tam. "Can I leave my contact details with you in case you find any new evidence?"

"Go ahead."

As Tam wrote down his number on a scrap of paper, Perry hovered near the door, tapping her foot impatiently. I had my doubts she intended to head meekly back to the inn. I'd bet the team intended to do some investigating of their own… and so did I.

5

I left the police station along with the Wardens, mostly to avoid another run-in with Petra on the way out. I could feel her stare on my back, magnified by her glasses, but I didn't turn around to acknowledge her. I knew Drew was doing his best, but I couldn't help feeling a little irked that the Wardens had waltzed into the office with less resistance than I'd encountered whenever I'd tried to help the police in the past—even if the outcome had ultimately been the same.

As the door closed behind us, I turned to Tam. "Your team isn't going to do anything inadvisable like sneak off to look at the body, are you?"

"Certainly not." When the vampire made a sceptical noise, Tam gave him a pointed look. "We play by the rules, Maurice. You know that."

"She doesn't." Maurice indicated me. "She's already thinking of sending her ghostly brother to have a poke around."

"How—?" I broke off. He hadn't heard me say to the others that Mart was my brother, and while I might have assumed the others had told him, there was another ability vampires had that I'd completely forgotten: mind reading. The sneaky vampire had been reading my thoughts since we'd met. *How* had I forgotten that basic detail about the undead?

Maurice bared his teeth in a grin. "You're not very bright for a Reaper, are you?"

"For a *what?*" Perry asked.

My heart plummeted. Farley's jaw dropped, and even Tam looked taken aback to hear of my Reaper status. *As if plucking the secrets out of my head wasn't enough.* Turning the full power of my Reaper glare onto the vampire, I snarled, "Get *out* of my head, or else I'll have every ghost in town team up to chase you out. Your friends too."

"Hey, that's not fair," Callum protested. "We weren't reading your thoughts. Also, Maurice, I thought you didn't do that anymore."

The vampire glared right back at me. "I do when I'm dealing with someone who sends her ghostly brother to spy on me."

"I didn't send him to spy on you. You brought that on yourself when you insulted our staff," I told him. "Besides, I'll respect your privacy if you respect mine. If you've been reading my thoughts, you deserve any trouble my brother gives you."

"That's enough," said Tam. "Maurice, we've talked about this. Reaper or not, she has the right to privacy."

Farley rocked back on her heels, her face pale, but her expression was more confused than afraid. "She doesn't look like a Reaper."

"That's because she's only half—" Maurice broke off when Mart appeared behind him and, without as much as a word, stuck both his hands through the vampire's chest. "Hey!"

Surprised my brother had come to my defence, I jabbed a

finger at Maurice. "I might be half Reaper, but my magic is as strong as a full one's, and it's perfectly within my powers to call on every ghost within hearing distance to chase you off if you cross any more lines."

Mart withdrew his hands and gave a rude gesture to the vampire. "That's right."

"Drop it, Maurice," said Perry, watching me with a mixture of intrigue and amusement. "I don't want to make an enemy of a Reaper. Do you?"

"She's no threat to me," said the vampire, but some of the heat had gone out of his voice. "I was only trying to warn you in case she tried to reap your souls."

I snorted. "As if. We wouldn't have many visitors at the inn if we made a habit of stealing the souls of our guests."

"Precisely," said Tam. "Have some common sense, Maurice. No practising Reaper would run ghost tours for a living."

"I'm not a practising Reaper, but we do have one of those, and he lives right next to the morgue." I pointed in that direction. "Just in case anyone was thinking of sneaking around to look at the body."

"That wasn't the plan," said Tam. "We planned to search the river, actually."

"Did we?" asked Callum.

"Pretty sure the police will have people looking around there for the other bodies," I said, "but if you *did* want to know what's up at the morgue, feel free to check in with me after my brother's had time to look around."

I nodded to Mart, who grinned back, but the vampire's scowl returned. "You have some nerve lecturing *me* about crossing lines."

"I never claimed to be a paragon of virtue," I said. "Unlike you, I don't have a boss to report to—except my employer at the inn, and she has no control over what I do when I'm not at work. Like I said, it's up to you. You're free to go it alone if you'd rather."

I figured Tam would stick to his rule book for the time being, and with the exception of the vampire, the others looked to him for instructions.

"We'll look around the river," he decided. "If we need anything, I'll be in touch, Maura."

"Sure." I needed to get back to work, though I figured I might as well have a poke around the river on the way back. "See you around."

After I parted ways with the Wardens, Mart glided alongside me down the high street. "I can go back to the morgue now to make sure that vampire doesn't sneak in when his teammates aren't looking."

"I don't really care if he does," I said. "It'll get him into trouble with Tam, which serves him right. No, I'm far more concerned that he'll blab my secrets to everyone he knows."

"I can push him into the river," Mart offered. "Vampires can't cross running water, remember?"

"Oh yeah." There was another trait I'd forgotten the undead possessed, along with the mind reading. "Wait, how'd he get to the inn without crossing the river?"

"Probably circled around the back," he said. "Vampires can move fast."

"True." I filed that one away to think about later. "All right. If you do see the vampire hanging around the morgue, let me know, won't you?"

"After I push him in the river."

"Nah, don't bother," I told him. "Tam might be a rule follower, but the rest of the team strike me as more on the flexible side when it comes to obeying the authorities. It might not even be him who gets there first." Perry, for one, had the look of someone who'd sneaked into a morgue or two in her time.

"If you say so."

"Meet me back at the inn." I headed for the bridge, slowing my pace when I reached the river.

On the bridge, I looked down at the water's rushing currents. *Are the other missing people somewhere down there? Was this simply a human serial killer or something more?* I dragged my gaze from the water to look for the ghost I'd seen yesterday, but he didn't appear to be around today.

I hadn't got his name, so if he'd moved on, I wouldn't be able to question him about who he'd been searching for in the water. Regardless, the odds of the ghost being able to help us find the killer were low, so I returned to the inn to rescue Jia from the lunchtime rush.

———

Mart still hadn't come back by the time Carey returned from school, and neither had our guests. If they wanted to wander through damp fields in the rain, that was their choice to make, but what in the world was my brother doing? Hounding the vampire again? Checking a dead body for signs of foul play shouldn't take hours, and despite my efforts to push the matter to the back of my mind, the thoughts kept coming back. *What're the odds of it being a human serial killer, really? They wouldn't have sent the Wardens here for no reason.*

When Carey entered the restaurant, shaking water off her umbrella, Jia waved at her. "Hey, Carey. Come and cheer Maura up. She's been moping all afternoon."

"Why?" Carey took off her wet coat, while Casper came sprinting in and dove underneath the table in a wet huddle. "What's going on?"

"Nothing." I gave Jia a look, warning her not to give away too much. Carey didn't need to be distracted by a potential serial killer, human or otherwise, when she had a ghost tour to run in a few hours. "The weather's miserable, and our guests left a ton of mud on the floor earlier."

"The weather's always miserable." Carey crouched to scoop up her familiar and cast a drying spell on his damp fur. "Really, what's going on?"

"My brother went out earlier and hasn't come back," I evaded. "I figure he's got distracted following our guests."

"Are they out?" She set her schoolbag next to her chair, scattering more raindrops and causing Casper to mew in protest. "It's not pleasant weather for a walk."

"No, but they're..." I hesitated. "Obsessive hikers. Ready for the ghost tour?"

Carey did not look entirely fooled at my change of subject, but her expression brightened. "I can't wait. I bet everyone will be happy to stay indoors tonight, so we might get some last-minute bookings."

"Yeah." I watched the door. "If Mart shows his face before then."

"Why's he following the newcomers?" she asked. "He's never been that interested in our guests before."

"He got into a spat with the vampire." That, at least, was true. "Turns out the vampire can see ghosts and has no manners, so Mart has made it his mission to annoy the crap out of him."

Her nose wrinkled. "I forgot one of them was a vampire. Can't they read minds?"

"Yeah, which I forgot." I didn't mind letting my screw-up slip if it distracted from the real reasons for my fixation on our new guests. "That's another reason Mart has declared war on him."

"He read your mind?" Her eyes widened. "Does that mean he knows you're a Reaper?"

I waged a mental battle for a moment and then opted for honesty. "Yes, but I don't think he's going to tell tales on me. I was more annoyed at the intrusion than anything else."

"I guess." Biting her lip, she scooped her familiar into her arms. "I hope they aren't on the ghost tour if he's going to ruin everything."

"He wouldn't." *I hope not.* If the Wardens remained out all evening, the vampire wouldn't be around to cause trouble on the tour, but there were no guarantees. Maurice had agreed not to poke into my thoughts, but he hadn't agreed not to mess with me in other ways, and ruining our tour was just the kind of underhanded tactic he'd use.

Hoping that the rest of the team would keep him occupied, I returned to work, but as the evening's tour drew ever closer with no signs of my brother, I started to wonder if he'd run into trouble.

"He's probably fine," Jia said when I mentioned this to her. "You can always summon him back."

"Nah, that'd freak out the other ghosts. Not to mention the guests."

"True." She cast a glance around the restaurant. "I don't think he'd want to skip the tour. He'll be back."

"Not if he's… I don't know… trapped or something."

"By that vampire?" Despite her sceptical tone, I knew that like me, she'd thought of the time the new coven leader had sneakily laid a trap in her office and left my brother imprisoned in a circle of sage. "I wouldn't have thought the rest of the team would have let him do anything like that."

"Hmm." I looked up sharply as the door blew inward, and to my relief, Mart himself came into the restaurant. "About time."

Mart sneezed loudly enough to rattle the glasses on the nearby tables, pretended to shake himself like a wet dog, and came gliding over to the bar as if he were on an ice rink. "It's nasty out there."

"Where have you been?" I asked, forgetting to keep my voice down. Several customers turned our way, and so did Carey.

"You know where I've been," he said. "I thought you wanted me to keep an eye out for trouble."

"I thought you'd got trapped." I beckoned him behind the bar. "And that you were going to be late for the tour."

"I'm not late. I'm early."

"Technically true," said Jia. "Where were you, though? It shouldn't have taken that long to look at a body. Unless the Wardens were there too?"

"The vampire tried," he said. "His leader stopped him. Then they went trekking around the river, looking for more bodies."

"Fun way to spend an afternoon," Jia commented. "Did they find anything?"

"Nope," said Mart. "The vampire gave them the slip, and he wasn't happy when I followed him."

"I didn't ask you to stalk the vampire," I whispered, conscious of Carey's eyes on me, though she could only hear my side of the conversation. "I thought he'd trapped you in sage or something. What did he do?"

"Oh, nothing interesting," he said. "Hunted more rats, mostly."

"Then why'd you spend all afternoon following him?" asked Jia.

"Because," he said, "the witch whose body they found in the river had bite marks on her neck."

My mouth fell open. "You what?"

Next to me, Jia goggled at him too. "Bite marks?"

"You heard me," he said. "I went to the morgue first, like you asked, and the body was laid out on a table. I'm guessing no one else has given her a thorough examination, because it was easy to spot the bite marks. Two of them, right here." He tapped his own transparent neck with his fingertips.

Bite marks on her neck? That was standard vampire behaviour, but hadn't the others said Maurice didn't feed on humans? And he'd spent the afternoon hunting rats… unless he'd been trying to cover his tracks.

"I figured that someone ought to make sure our vampire friend didn't claim another victim," added Mart. "You're welcome."

"But they weren't even in town when…" *When she'd disappeared.* Not to mention that the other missing persons had vanished several days ago—but I couldn't say any more with an audience. "Okay, I'll talk to them when they come back. Whereabouts were they when you last saw them?"

"They were going to get dinner," he replied. "Their fanged friend had joined them, so I figured he wasn't going to sneak off again."

"They weren't interested in coming back here?" I guessed they'd spent enough time at the inn already, and I wouldn't complain about them skipping out on the ghost tour. "All right. Thanks for… for keeping an eye on them."

We would need to have a proper discussion later without anyone listening in, but for now, I sent a message to Drew, letting him know what Mart had discovered. Then I did my best to put the matter to the back of my thoughts.

Not that Carey was so easily fooled. "Why were you so shocked at what your brother told you? What's going on?"

"It… It turns out the vampire hunts rats instead of biting people." I didn't know if that qualified as shocking enough to explain my reaction, but it was the first thing that popped into my head. "It wasn't a pleasant mental image, let me tell you."

Her brow scrunched up. "Weird."

"Mart thought he might try biting someone," Jia put in.

"That's why he followed the vampire. Turns out he's a vegetarian. Or the vampire equivalent."

"Casper chased off all the rats near the inn," Carey said. "That's probably why he had to go looking elsewhere."

Hmm. The town had more of a ghost problem than a rat problem, but the bite marks on the dead body indicated that the vampire might not have been completely truthful about his diet choices. That, or there was a second bloodsucker in the area.

With less than an hour until our ghost tour started, I wouldn't be able to question the vampire myself, so I added a follow-up message to Drew and asked him to drop by the inn later if he had time. It was up to him if he wanted to tell the rest of the officers about the bite marks… without giving away that I was the one who'd let him know they were present. That would invite too many awkward questions.

At eight o'clock, the ghost tour kicked off. Carey stood at the foot of the stairs, microphone in hand, while the other guests filled the lobby. Mart joined the rest of the ghostly team as they put on their usual show for the guests, rattling windows and doors and—in Vicky's case—grabbing people's hands as she wove amongst the crowd.

Jia and I remained by the front doors, watching out for trouble, but the Wardens didn't make a return during the first part of the tour. When the group headed upstairs, Mart lingered behind with Jia and me.

"What are you doing?" I whispered to him, watching the last of the guests climbing the stairs. "Aren't you going upstairs?"

"I'm waiting for the vampire to come back, of course."

"Why?" I asked. "You said yourself you didn't see him doing anything that suggests he was involved in the attack on that witch." He didn't bite people… or so he claimed.

"I don't trust him."

"Neither do I, but we have to think of the guests." Jia beckoned to Mart. "Come upstairs with me. Maura will handle any…"

"Handle what?" The question came from Allie, who'd remained at the desk throughout the tour. "What's going on?"

"There might be an issue with one of our guests," I murmured to her. "You know that group of…"

"Wardens?" she finished. "I thought they had no connection to the other Wardens who visited us before."

"They don't," I said, "but one of them is a vampire, and Mart said he's been acting, erm… weirdly. What day did they arrive again?"

"Two days ago," she said. "Why?"

They were here before the witch died. But not, I thought, *before the other missing persons incidents. Unless the vampire had arrived ahead of them, but that would be difficult to prove.*

Before I could say another word, cold air gusted into my back as the front doors opened. The damp and bedraggled Wardens stepped into the lobby, talking amongst themselves. Allie's gaze went towards them, alarm flickering in her eyes, but I put on a reassuring tone. "Never mind. It's nothing."

I'd tell her about the bite marks later if they became relevant… which they might, given that from the furious way the vampire glared at me, he'd plucked the thought right out of my head.

6

Silence filled the lobby as the other Wardens noticed Maurice had stopped dead—pun intended. The vampire stood in the doorway, his teeth bared, his gaze fixed on me.

"What is it?" Tam asked him. "Maurice?"

"He just dived into my thoughts again," I supplied. "I assume he didn't like what he saw in there."

The vampire hissed between his teeth. "You can't expect me to ignore—"

"Maura?" Jia peered downstairs. "What's going on?"

"Stay with the guests. I'll be out there." I pointed towards the door. "We'll talk outside."

"In the rain?" Callum's complaint faded when Tam turned to face the rest of his team, a stern expression on his face.

"Outside," Tam said. "All of you. And, Maurice, if you run off, you'll have to answer to me."

Whoa. Tam couldn't read my mind, could he? No, he wasn't a vampire, but I wasn't entirely sure he was human either. In any case, even the vampire didn't voice an argument as the team followed their leader back outside the inn.

I didn't much like the idea of standing in the rain, but it was better than causing a scene in front of the other guests. As a gust of cold air blew into my face, I wrapped my arms around myself, wishing I'd had the sense to wear a coat.

Callum sighed at Maurice. "I told you not to read her thoughts again. Why—"

"She was about to accuse me of murder." The vampire's eyes glittered with anger as he looked me up and down. "Don't deny it."

"I wasn't." I really hadn't been, either. "But it's interesting that you'd jump to that conclusion."

"Don't try that," he growled. "Your brother's been following me around all afternoon."

"I didn't tell him to do that either. Mart does as he likes." I hoped he was too busy with the ghost tour to notice the clamour outside, but we'd have to keep this chat short to wrap it up before the other guests came downstairs. "I *did* send him to look around the morgue, and if he saw anything that gave him reason to follow you, that's not my problem."

He scoffed. "Really? Want me to make it your problem?"

"Maurice," said Tam. "*Did* you disobey me and read her thoughts?"

His jaw tensed. "She thinks *I* killed that witch."

Farley sucked in a breath, while Callum blinked in apparent genuine puzzlement. "Why would she think that?"

"There were bite marks on the witch's neck," I told the team. "I didn't say Maurice was the murderer, but we don't *have* any other vampires in town. It's only natural that my brother would want to check up on him."

"Yes, you do," said Maurice.

I blinked. "Come again?"

"You do have another vampire in town," he said. "I saw him when I was looking around the town yesterday evening."

"Where?" Was he bluffing? Pity I couldn't read *his*

thoughts, though I likely didn't want to be privy to any insults he was directing at me right now.

"I don't know, do I?" he said. "We can move much faster than anyone else, and the guy clearly didn't want to be seen."

"You're lying." My phone buzzed loudly. Drew was calling me. *Oh boy.* "Go on, spill it, vampire. What did you do?"

"I didn't do anything," said Maurice. "Your brother can confirm that himself."

"He wasn't with you for the past couple of hours, as you well know." When the buzzing continued, I answered the phone. "Drew?"

"Maura," he said. "There's a problem."

"Oh?"

"The witch's body has disappeared from the morgue. I don't suppose those new friends of yours have been there recently?"

I gripped the phone in my hand. "When did this happen?"

"In the past couple of hours."

"Right." I swung back to the vampire, shot him a glare, and continued speaking to Drew. "I don't suppose you have time to drop by the inn?"

"Now?" he asked. "Wait—do you have an idea of who was responsible?"

"Possibly yes." If I said outright that my number-one suspect was right in front of my face, the vampire would doubtless make a run for it, and even Tam and the rest of the team might not be able to catch him. "Is there a chance you can get away from your fellow officers and come here alone? The ghost tour is still going on, and we don't need all the other guests to realise what's going on."

He exhaled. "It'll be tricky, but I think I can pull it off. See you in a bit."

"Thanks, Drew." I ended the call.

Maurice wore the same defiant expression, but he hadn't

reacted to the news Drew had given me. Evidently, he'd obeyed his leader and hadn't delved into my thoughts this time.

"What is it?" asked Tam. "What happened?"

"The witch's body is missing," I said. "Specifically, the body with vampire bite marks on her neck vanished from the morgue in the past two hours. Know anything about that?"

"I don't have to listen to your accusations," Maurice cut in. "You called the police on me, did you?"

"The police called *me*," I corrected. "And no, I didn't mention you. I just asked Drew to come here to judge for himself."

"Why did you tell him to leave the other officers behind?" Tam's voice rang with tension, but he hadn't given his team any further instructions. From his intent expression, he wanted to hear from me first.

"Because I'm giving you the benefit of the doubt." Footsteps and raised voices drew my attention to the lobby. The guests were coming back downstairs for the end part of the ghost tour. *Oh no.*

A calculated smile crossed the vampire's face when he noticed. "Are you really?"

"We'll finish this later," I said. "When Drew shows up— and if you're as innocent as you say you are, you'll stick around and answer some questions. Oh, and without disturbing the ghost tour."

"I don't have to deal with this nonsense." Maurice veered towards the door, but luckily, Tam stepped into his way before I had to intervene myself.

"None of that," said Tam. "We're guests here, and if you acted like a rational person, maybe Maura wouldn't be inclined to suspect you."

"He's got you there," said Perry. "Calm down. And leave the humans alone."

The vampire rolled his eyes at her but remained beside his teammates: Farley, who'd gone as tense as a wire; Callum, who wore a placating look; and Perry, who looked as if she wouldn't mind thwacking him on the head herself. As for Tam, I liked his pragmatic approach, but I couldn't count on him not to jump to his friend's defence if the vampire turned out to be involved in the witch's death.

Through the doors, I saw the guests follow Carey into the restaurant for the tour's end, but Mart spotted our group outside and abandoned his fellow ghosts to come out and join us.

"What's all this?" He drifted through the front door, sticking out his tongue at the vampire. "Weird place for a meeting."

"The witch's body went missing from the morgue," I told him. "Drew's on his way to ask some questions."

"He's wasting his time," the vampire muttered.

"Also, Maurice claims he's not the only vampire in town," I added. "Apparently, another one showed up for the sole purpose of murdering random citizens."

My brother gave a laugh. "Yeah, right. I'd know if there was another bloodsucker sniffing around."

Maurice's hands clenched. "I won't stand for being insulted. I'm telling the truth. I didn't kill that girl."

"Then where'd the body go?" I countered. "Assuming someone didn't steal it, bodies don't tend to disappear of their own accord. Unless they're not as dead as they look, and I can think of exactly two reasons that might be the case."

"The vampiric transformation process takes much longer than a day," Maurice spat. "Even a washed-up ex-Reaper like you ought to know that."

"All right, enough from you." I did my best to reel in my temper. "You aren't doing a great job of proving your own innocence."

"You've already decided I'm guilty despite the facts," he shot back at me.

"Like I said, I'm giving you the benefit of the doubt. Doesn't mean I have to be nice to someone who has fewer manners than a rampaging manticore."

He was right, though. Vampires slept for around seventy-two hours before they transformed. Unless the process had been accelerated somehow, the witch hadn't been mid-transformation when her body had disappeared. Not to mention Maurice would have done a runner if he really had been behind the attack. No way would he have come back to the inn with the rest of his team.

And while the missing witch's body had been found, the same wasn't true of the other missing persons... who'd vanished before the Wardens had arrived at the inn. As I'd said to Maurice, there were two options, and if the witch hadn't turned into a vampire, the second possibility was that her body had risen as a zombie.

That would mean another necromancer was in the area.

I kept the second theory to myself for now. Given his lack of reaction, Maurice didn't read my mind, either, but we endured an unpleasant few minutes of waiting in the rain before Drew showed up. He approached the inn as the guests were beginning to disperse after the ghost tour, water running off his coat and his dark-brown hair dripping wet.

I waved at him from around the side of the inn, where Tam and the others had huddled under an overhang to shelter from the rain. "Sorry I dragged you over here."

"You have no idea how hard it was for me to ditch Petra," he said. "I had to put her in charge of the team I sent to the morgue to stop her from following me here."

That figured. "She'd do well to remember I helped in another case that was awfully similar to this one."

"Similar?" His brow furrowed. "In what way? The body is missing—wait, you mean like Mr. Cogman?"

I grimaced at the memory of the grumpy ghost whose body had become a shambling corpse after his death. "Possibly. Were there signs that the morgue had been broken into?"

"Actually… no," he replied. "The guy working there said he locked the door, but nobody appeared to have tampered with it from the outside."

"So there's a chance the body might have walked off of its own accord instead of being stolen."

"It might well have." He surveyed the Wardens' huddled group. "*Have* any of you been to the morgue since we last spoke?"

"No," answered Tam. "We kept our word and stayed away from the body. If it's missing—stolen or otherwise—none of us was involved."

"There's one slight problem," I added to Drew. "The bite marks. Did you tell anyone else?"

"No." Drew followed my gaze to Maurice. "I haven't had personal experience with vampires, and neither have most of my fellow officers, but certain members of my team would be disinclined to overlook the possible connection to our visitors if they were to discover that the body had bite marks on her neck."

Maurice bared his teeth in a scowl. "I didn't go anywhere near that girl."

"He claims there's another vampire in town," I explained. "You'd know if there was, wouldn't you?"

"Not necessarily." Drew frowned. "Did you see another? Where?"

"By the cemetery," Maurice replied. "He moved too fast

for me to see his face, but no other paranormal can match a vampire for speed."

"Maybe he saw Harold the Reaper," Mart suggested.

"Who? Maurice or the other vampire?" I'd thought my brother was all in on blaming Maurice, though I didn't know if another vampire being in town was better or worse than a repeat of the zombie incident. To Maurice, I added, "Also, how do you know it's a 'he' if you didn't see his face?"

"I don't," said Maurice. "I guessed. It was dark at the time. That was yesterday."

Hmm. "I have a hard time believing Harold the Reaper wouldn't have spotted an intruder. He's the official Reaper, and he probably knew you were nosing around his graveyard too."

"That old guy is a Reaper?" Maurice snorted. "And to think I almost believed you when you said he was dangerous."

"I wouldn't underestimate him." I returned my attention to Drew. "Did you see the body yourself? Or speak to the forensic team?"

"No, they didn't have time to properly examine the body before it vanished," he replied. "About two hours ago."

"Maurice was with us the whole time," said Tam. "And like he said, the vampire transformation process takes several days. The girl has been dead for less than a day. Is that right?"

"Correct." Drew gave him a level stare. "I took a risk by bringing your team into my office. Don't give me cause to regret it."

"We won't." Tam drew in a breath. "I don't believe the body has risen as a vampire, but we've dealt with similar situations before, and if you'll allow us to have a look around the morgue, one of us might be able to figure out if anyone tampered with it."

I looked to Drew, who shook his head. "I've already sent a team there. They aren't likely to appreciate interference."

Not least because he'd put Petra in charge. To Tam, I said, "I'd like to hear about these 'similar situations' you've been in. Did they involve the body walking away by itself?"

"We can't discuss past missions with outsiders," Tam said. "That said, I imagine you're familiar with some of the possibilities yourself. Didn't you mention a second theory?"

He doesn't miss much, this guy. "Yeah. My second theory is that the body turned into a zombie. They don't have a seventy-two-hour lead time."

Farley blanched, but the rest of the team didn't react with much more than mild surprise.

"You've dealt with the undead before?" asked Perry.

"Yes, I have," I said. "Recently, in fact. If a necromancer put a spell on the body, the zombie would have returned to their side the instant they gave the command."

"Everyone knows how zombies work," said Maurice. "They're easy to deal with."

"Necromancers aren't," I told him. "I handled the last one I ran into, but if you think this is a necromancer's work, I'd appreciate your cooperation."

"It's one possibility," said Perry with a glance at Tam. "Right?"

"If there have been necromancers in town before, it certainly is," Tam said. "There are other possibilities, including that the body was taken by the killer or by someone else, but if the door to the morgue wasn't opened from outside…"

"That's my understanding," Drew said, "but the team has yet to examine the scene for any use of magic or other inter-ference."

"And there's only so much human eyes can see," Maurice

added, his eyes glittering with amusement. "The authorities are stumbling around in the dark."

"Wise words to say to someone with the power to arrest you," Mart quipped, though he knew as well as I did that Maurice was right. The police *did* have their limits, and I'd run up against them more than once in the past.

"I take it they wouldn't appreciate me showing up?" I already knew the answer to that one. "Even to look around outside for any ghosts who might have seen the body?"

Drew's brows crept upward. "You want to go to the scene yourself?"

"I know Petra doesn't want me there, but she can't stop me from looking outside for any trail the zombie might have left behind, can she?"

"No…" His gaze flickered to the Wardens. "That said, I doubt she'd appreciate me bringing a crowd of onlookers."

Perry made a noise of frustration. "If Maura gets to go there, why not us? The zombie might still be wandering around."

"It might," I said, surprised the others had jumped on board with my zombie theory so readily. Even if it did turn out to be a vampire instead, I'd be hard-pressed to take on a vamp single-handedly, so having backup wouldn't be the worst idea. "Petra doesn't want to deal with another zombie incident, does she?"

Drew sighed. "It's your risk to take."

Tam cleared his throat. "I'm not intending to step on any toes. If my team and I aren't welcome at the morgue, we'll leave."

Maurice made a noise of disdain but didn't contradict him aloud. Perry looked almost excited at the prospect of fighting a zombie, but she was the only one who did. Farley and Callum wore resigned expressions, as if they would rather have gone to bed.

"Sounds fair to me," I ventured. "Give me a second to grab my coat first."

Not that it would make much difference, given that the rain had soaked through to my skin, but I seized on the chance to dart indoors and flag down Allie to tell her I was going out.

Jia took the news with a resigned shake of her head. "Zombies *again?*"

"It might not be," I said over my shoulder as I came running downstairs wearing my waterproof coat. "But I'd rather keep that vampire where I can see him."

"Wise idea." Jia waved goodbye as the doors to the inn closed behind me.

Drew waited for me outside. "You're determined to do this?"

"Yes," I answered for everyone. "If there's a zombie running around, I'd rather get it under our control, especially given that we have at least two other missing persons who may or may not be in the same condition."

His expression darkened. "I don't think the rest of my team is going to take me up on that theory without proof."

"Maybe remind Petra of the last time she had to deal with a necromancer," I said to him. "She was in over her head then, and it's the same now."

"Necromancer." Perry shuddered. "We don't have a pleasant track record with those."

"That makes two of us." I pulled up my hood. "Let's go."

7

A nighttime walk in the rain was not my idea of fun, let alone with a grumpy vampire for company. While I doubted the wisdom of bringing Maurice back to the scene of the crime, if he was right about there being a second vampire in town, what better way to fight him off than with a vamp of our own?

Not that there was a high chance of him being right. Why would another vampire have decided to move to Hawkwood Hollow without announcing his presence to anyone? I'd lived here for months and never seen one, and vampires were generally creatures of the night. I'd spent no small amount of time sneaking around in the late hours, so I thought I'd have run into another resident bloodsucker.

Mart accompanied us to the bridge and then waved goodbye. "Have fun getting drenched in the rain."

"You're not coming with us?"

"I don't like zombies, remember?"

"We don't know if that's what we're dealing with." Mart's ability to fight off monsters was limited, so I didn't mind him staying behind at the inn. "If you see anything weird at the inn, you'll come and warn me, won't you?"

"By 'weird,' I assume you don't mean Wade's break-dancing?"

"Definitely not." I watched his retreat to the inn and then hastened to cross the bridge and catch up with the others. On the way over the river, I had one last look around for the ghost I'd seen the previous day, but the rain and darkness made it even harder to see a transparent figure than it already was.

Drew waited beside the bridge. "Everything okay?"

"Sure… Where's Maurice?" The other Wardens had reached the other side of the river, but the vampire was nowhere to be seen.

Where'd he sneak off to?

"He can't cross running water," Tam said. "He'll meet us on the other side."

"We're already there." I gestured to the bridge behind us. "Guess that's the last we'll see of him."

At least it was one less person for me to keep an eye on, though we might get into trouble if the rest of the police found out we'd both found *and* lost a potential suspect.

"If there *is* another vampire, he'll come back and help us fight them off," Callum said confidently.

I had my doubts, and Maurice did not rejoin us when we reached the main high street. After we crossed the road to the morgue next to the cemetery, Drew approached an officer standing outside and spoke in a low voice, while I hung back with the Wardens. The officer was too busy trying to hold an umbrella upright to notice our group. Evidently, he'd drawn the short straw and been forced to stand outside in the rain to keep watch while the rest of the officers went into the morgue. When he stepped aside to let Drew in, I heard Petra's voice inside, shrill and complaining. That figured.

I turned to the Wardens, who were conversing in low voices. "I doubt you'll get inside."

"We're splitting up," Tam murmured back. "Does the morgue have a back entrance?"

"Yeah, but the officers will be watching that too," I replied. "There's hardly enough room in there for the police, let alone your team."

"That's why we won't all go," he said. "Farley, you should come with me. Callum, Perry, do you two want to look for any signs of the witch's body?"

"No thanks," said Callum. "Shouldn't one of us wait for Maurice?"

"*You* can," said Perry. "I'd rather handle the zombie. If there is one."

"Not alone," Tam said firmly. "All right, you two stay together. If Maurice comes back, he knows where to find us."

I cleared my throat. "I'm going to look for the missing witch. Anyone who wants to come with me is welcome to." *Unless they're a vampire, that is.*

"Are you?" Perry tilted her head on one side. "Tam, how about I go with her? Callum can wait for Maurice. I know he'd rather do that than fight a zombie."

I'm not part of your team. I squashed down my annoyance. Perry wasn't the worst of her group, and I had to admit that the idea of having someone to watch my back wasn't unappealing—especially someone who could see ghosts and who looked like she could hold her own in a fight.

Tam studied us both, his green eyes bright in the darkness. "If you're both okay with that plan."

I shrugged. "I am."

"And me." Perry bounced on the balls of her feet. "Shall we be off?"

"Sure, but watch out for the Reaper." I indicated the graveyard near the morgue. "I wasn't kidding when I said he's not fond of people disturbing him."

"Including you?" She pulled out her wand and conjured up a small flame to light the way through the rainy darkness. "He'll want to know if there's a zombie wandering around, won't he?"

"Not unless it's literally on his doorstep." I pulled out my own wand and conjured a light. "I doubt it'll be this close to the morgue, though. Someone would have spotted it wandering around."

"Hmm." She was silent for a moment as we paced down the street, and I could see her mind ticking over the possibilities. "Do you really think the witch turned into a zombie?"

"If she's not a vampire, a zombie is the second-most-likely option," I said. "If it turns out your friend was right about there being a second vampire in town, I'll stand corrected, but I have my doubts."

"I don't think it's a vampire either," said Perry. "Also, Maurice is not my friend."

"Is he coming back, do you think?"

"Hard to tell." She drew in a breath. "I can say he's not the person responsible for killing that witch, though. I've lived with him for a month and never known him to bite any humans. He might be an obnoxious twit, but he's not a murderer. I had my doubts about him at first, so I learned that the hard way."

"Ah." A month? She'd been with the team for less time than I'd thought, and it would explain the tense vibes between her and the vampire. "What would make you assume there isn't a second vampire?"

"Instinct," she replied. "There'd be other bite victims… people with gaps in their memories. Someone would have noticed in a town as small as this one."

Hmm. Had she hunted a vampire before? If so, that must have been an awkward conversation to have with her new housemate. I shined the light of my wand along the pavement and the fence bordering the graveyard, but the only movement I saw was the officer letting Tam into the morgue.

Perry shook her head. "Honestly. He can get in anywhere."

"Lucky for him," I remarked.

"Doesn't dating the head of the police get you some concessions?"

"Not according to some people," I said. "Most of the police officers can't see ghosts, and they're disinclined to let outsiders muscle in on their investigations and bring in witnesses they can't communicate with themselves. Drew started out like that, too, but he's got better."

"I should hope so if you're dating one another." She lifted her head when Callum and Farley approached us. "I take it the rest of us aren't allowed in?"

"There's not much room in there," Farley replied. "Besides, they're just debating over which door the thief used."

"The police think the body was stolen?" I asked. "Didn't they learn their lesson from the zombie incident?"

"Don't ask me," said Farley. "Actually, Callum said he might be able to track the missing witch by scent."

"He can?" I turned to the werewolf. "Can you pick up her scent?"

"Possibly." He sniffed. "Not out here. All I can smell is the rain and something rotten."

"Well, we are near a graveyard and a building full of corpses," said Perry. "You think you can find her, though?"

"If he can, so can Drew," I replied. "He's a werewolf too."

"He is?" Perry nodded in understanding. "I guess he can't really shift into a wolf while working, though..."

"He doesn't like doing that, no." He'd only shifted a handful of times, most of which had involved him helping me fight off various monsters, which wasn't the least likely outcome of the night. "Can you sniff her out in your human form?"

"Possibly," said Callum. "It won't do much good if I find her and can only communicate in growls. I need to find the start of the trail first."

As he approached the morgue, a cold breeze brought a rotten stench to my nostrils. *Ew.*

Did the smell mean the zombie was close? No—the witch had only been dead a day. She wouldn't have decayed that fast. I sniffed again, shining my wand's light around, and spied movement on the other side of the cemetery's fence.

A sudden, familiar chill seized me. The afterworld.

Is that Harold? No—he never used his abilities. I sprinted for the gate, letting myself into the cemetery.

"Get out of my house!" bellowed old Harold. "Get away!"

What's he doing? Once through the gate, I ran towards the Reaper's small cottage, at first unable to see what he'd deemed a big enough threat to come out of his house. A closer look revealed he wasn't holding his weapon, though the shadows circling his hands made him look menacing enough that he was hardly recognisable as the lazy Reaper who'd hung up his cloak decades ago.

Then my gaze landed on the transparent shaking form in front of him. Not a zombie but a ghost.

"Wait!" I skidded to a halt behind the spirit. "What are you doing?"

"What do you think?" Harold asked. "This spirit invaded my home."

"Why?" I directed my question at the ghost, who shrank away from me. Despite the darkness surrounding the area, he had a familiar face.

Wait. It was the ghost from the bridge. The ghost I'd thought had disappeared.

"I need your help, Reaper," he said tremulously.

My brows shot up. "You know, you could have asked for my help the last time I saw you."

"That was before *she* came back."

"She?" I echoed. "You were looking for someone in the river... I don't suppose it was the same witch whose body they found earlier today?"

He flinched, which was answer enough, and shrank back even farther into the shadows.

"Her body disappeared," I went on. "Where'd she go?"

The ghost lifted his head, terror flashing in his eyes. "I'm sorry!"

"Sorry for what?"

To my alarm, the Reaper lifted his hands. Shadows flowed from Harold's palms and enveloped the ghostly figure.

The spirit let out a single high-pitched screech. When the dark faded, the ghost was gone.

"Dammit." I whipped around to face Harold. "Did you have to?"

"I didn't do anything." He grunted. "The afterworld called him back, as well it should."

With a satisfied expression, he retreated into his house, and the door closed behind him.

"Thanks for nothing." The back of my neck prickled, and the stark terror on the ghost's face entered my mind again.

I spun around, heart lurching when I saw movement, but it was only Perry. She walked into view, her gaze fixed on the Reaper's house. "What was that about?"

"Never mind." Had the ghost been staring at her? Or had his terror been more to do with the Reaper's presence? "You almost met our other friendly neighbourhood Reaper."

"I thought you said not to go near his house." She trod closer to me. "Who was that ghost?"

"Absolutely no idea." I drew in a breath and regretted it when the stench of rot filled my nostrils. Coughing, I turned my back on the Reaper's house. "What *is* that smell?"

"I was wondering the same," Perry commented. "It smells like death… which I guess isn't that unusual for a morgue. Did that ghost know the murder victim?"

She must have heard more of our conversation than I'd thought. "Possibly, but thanks to the Reaper, I can't call him back and check."

"Isn't his job to banish ghosts?"

"He doesn't take his responsibilities all that seriously." I turned my back and paced away from the cottage, and Perry walked at my side. "Most of the time."

"Don't worry. I won't tell Maurice." She gave me a sideways look. "I've not seen a Reaper up close before. I didn't know he could banish a ghost without a scythe."

"The ghost half banished himself," I said. "Old Harold does have a scythe, but he uses it to hang his coats on."

Perry snorted. "Wow, he's a character. I was just curious. I've banished plenty of ghosts myself… the non-Reaper way, that is."

"I figured." Maybe that accounted for the spirit's reaction to her, but she didn't look like anything other than human to my eyes. "And zombies?"

"Not for a while," she replied. "That ghost didn't drop any clues?"

"Nope, but I saw him yesterday." I figured it couldn't hurt to tell her at this point. "On the bridge. He looked as if he was calling out to someone in the water, but he took off when he caught me watching."

Her brow wrinkled. "Was he looking for Elaine Langley?"

"Who?"

"The witch who drowned," she said. "I heard her name from the police. Do you think he was calling to her ghost?"

"I don't have the faintest idea." I paused in mid-step. "You know what? I'm going to try to get more details from the Reaper first."

I turned on my heel and walked up to the door to the Reaper's cottage.

"What're you doing?" Perry caught up to me, her gaze flickering over the curtained windows and the number 42 fixed to the door. "I thought you said he didn't want to talk to you."

"I'm going to try my usual tactic of annoying Harold until he gives me an explanation."

"What's your success rate?"

"Not spectacular." I knocked twice, and then the door swung inward on my third attempt.

The Reaper loomed over me with his scythe in his grip.

I was so startled that I tripped over my feet and skidded in the mud, coming to an undignified halt next to Perry. Catching my balance, I stared at the Reaper. "What? Are you going to Reap *my* soul now?"

"I might," he growled. "What do you want?"

"I—" My gaze caught on his scythe. "Why do you have that? Were you expecting to use it?"

He gave me a look that implied I was dense for asking, which only served to heighten my suspicions. I did my best to pull myself together. "What did that ghost tell you? He was on the bridge yesterday—he knew the victim, didn't he? The witch whose body the police found in the river."

"You didn't need to disturb me to find out something you already knew." He made to close the door, but I stuck my foot in the way.

"That's not all I want to know." I angled myself so he couldn't slam the door on my foot. "The body is missing, and we're pretty sure it's wandering around as a zombie. Is that why he asked for your help?"

He ignored my question, eyeing Perry. "And just who are you?"

"Perry." She lifted her chin. "I'm with the Wardens. Are you Hawkwood Hollow's Reaper?"

He lowered the scythe. "You two share the same talent for asking questions you already know the answer to. If the Wardens are here, I won't be needed."

"What's that supposed to mean?" Perry asked. "You *were* going to hunt down the ghost's friend?"

Instead of answering her, Harold shoved the door into the side of my foot and knocked me sideways. Perry caught my arm to stop me from falling over, and when I turned back to the cottage, the door was shut.

"Ow."

"What's his problem?" She released my arm and walked up to the cottage window, but the curtains were drawn, revealing nothing but a liberal coating of dust and a few spiders.

"Don't worry. He does that to everyone." I lifted my foot gingerly, but I didn't think he'd left a bruise.

"He wouldn't need a scythe to deal with a zombie, I don't think," she observed. "Unless he expected to run into the necromancer who created it."

"He might have." I sniffed, the rotting scent reaching my nose again. "Wish I'd asked *where* the zombie was hiding."

"It can't have gone far." Perry squinted into the darkness around the cottage. "Might it be in the graveyard?"

"It shouldn't have stuck around this close to the morgue." I lifted my wand, using my light charm to illuminate the area behind the Reaper's house. "It's worth looking around."

It weirded me out that the Reaper had decided to pick up his own scythe rather than sit back and let me deal with it the way he usually did. Yes, he hadn't known the Wardens were in town, but it was a bizarrely proactive decision on his part. Had he figured out something else he hadn't told us?

Another gust of wind brought the same decaying stench into our faces. Perry made a low, disgusted noise. "Okay, someone needs to close the freezer door in there."

"I don't think it's coming from the morgue." I swivelled on my heel then paced down the shadowy path behind the Reaper's cottage.

Was the smell from the zombie? Surely not—the witch hadn't been dead long enough. But if the other missing persons had turned into undead, too, maybe they'd arrived to welcome their newest recruit.

"Not a smart move, that," I muttered to myself, shining my wand's light up and down the path. "Bringing your zombies this close to a Reaper's house."

"Huh?" Perry followed close behind me. "You think the other zombies are here as well?"

"It would explain the smell." I didn't need a shifter's senses to track the direction the wind came from, and Perry and I followed the path deeper into the cemetery with the damp stench steering us towards our target.

A shuffling noise amid the graves drew me to a halt.

"Where is it?" I shined the light onto the tombstones where I'd heard the noise. "Show yourself."

Silence answered. Then a shadowy body rose from behind the row of stones.

8

The body stood hunched over behind the graves, emanating the stench of decay. I wrinkled my nose, holding my wand aloft as I moved closer. It didn't *look* like the last zombie I'd seen, but even my wand's light had trouble piercing the curtain of drizzle that hung over the gravestones to make out its features.

Perry sucked in a breath and coughed. "I don't think that's a zombie."

"If not, what is it?" I shined the light directly over the figure, which wore the tattered remains of a jacket and jeans. Long, stringy hair hung in curtains around a pointed face with razor-sharp teeth, while its hands ended in long claws with filthy nails. *Okay, that's not a zombie.*

The monster shrieked. The piercing noise caused both of us to recoil. My feet skidded back in the mud, and I caught my balance against a gravestone, my wand flying from my hand.

"Ack." I scanned the darkness at my feet for my wand, but the light spell must have gone out when I dropped it. *Dammit.*

Perry backed up to my side. "That's not a zombie. It's a ghoul."

A ghoul? I hadn't seen one outside of a textbook, but the greyish skin and sharp claws definitely didn't belong to a zombie. "I think this might be what that ghost was trying to warn the Reaper about."

Which means... which means this monster was Elaine Langley.

Perry lifted her wand. "Haven't seen a ghoul in a few years. Nasty creatures."

No kidding. Ghouls feasted on the dead, which would explain why this one was in a graveyard, but they could be downright dangerous to living people as well. *How did poor Elaine end up turning into this monster?*

As the ghoul slithered and crawled towards us, Perry flicked her wand, casting a spell that froze the monster in midmotion.

"That won't hold it forever." She backed up a step, shining her wand's light amid the graves. "I can't see your wand—"

The ghoul gave a rattling growl and shook itself slowly, as if trying to dislodge the spell Perry had flung at it.

I swore. "Since when can they shake off freeze-frame spells?"

"They're pretty resilient." Perry backed away, holding her wand aloft. "Use your Reaper powers."

Well, now. I didn't take kindly to being given orders, and while I didn't say so aloud, my silence must have spoken for itself. With a hint of guilt, Perry whispered, "Sorry, I'm used to working in a team... Never thought I'd say that."

"It was a good suggestion anyway." I lifted my free hand and called the afterworld as the ghoul lunged forward, shaking off the remnants of the freeze-frame spell.

The shadows flew from my grip when the ghoul hit me like a battering ram. Perry and I both went flying backwards, and while she managed to land in a roll and come upright in a crouch, I wasn't as athletic as her. My back hit the ground, the air rushing from my lungs. Breathless, I looked up at the ghoul's rotting face and rolled to the side when its claws plunged downward. That monster moved way too fast for something that looked like it should have been slow and clumsy, and the mud and rain made it a struggle to get back on my feet.

Perry, who'd managed to keep hold of her wand, conjured up a dazzling light. I squeezed my eyes shut, and the beast yowled, repelled by the brightness. While it was distracted, I rolled upright, hand over my eyes to shield my sight. I had even less chance of spotting my wand while half blinded, but the darkness of the afterworld answered my call, swirling around my hand.

"Get out of here." When the ghoul slithered towards us like a particularly ugly serpent, I hit out. The beast ducked behind a grave, and the shadows bounced harmlessly off the stone. "Since when did they move so damn fast?"

"An evolutionary advantage to make up for them being hideous?" Perry lifted her wand. "Close your eyes."

Brightness ignited for a second time, and I saw that the ghoul had dug a massive hole behind the row of graves, which was what it must have been doing when we'd interrupted. Looking for its next meal, I guessed. *Ugh.*

The ghoul lunged, its clawed feet kicking up the soil. A wave of dirt hit both of us, and Perry's wand's light dimmed as she was forced to shield her face. I coughed, spitting out soil, and I could hear Perry swearing behind me. I ran forward, but by the time I scrubbed the dirt out of my eyes enough to see, the ghoul's shadow had vanished amid the graves.

"Where the hell did it go?" Perry spun on her heel, cursing under her breath. "Bloody monster."

I finally spied my wand lying on the ground and grabbed

it, casting another light spell. But even with two beams of light cutting through the night, the ghoul was nowhere to be seen. *Where did it go?* The stench it had left in its wake was overwhelming no matter which way I turned, which made it impossible to tell which direction it had fled in.

Perry flicked a handful of dirt out of her hair. "It must have figured it had no chance against the two of us and bolted for its lair."

"The question is where is that?" I shined the wand's light over the mess of damp mud it'd left behind the graves. "I suppose it'll be easy to find if we follow the stench."

"If there's more than one ghoul inside the lair, we'll need backup." Perry backed away from the graves. "Would your friendly local Reaper be willing to volunteer to help us?"

"I wouldn't bet on it." After casting a last searching light over the area and finding no remaining clues, I made for the path towards the Reaper's cottage.

Old Harold's door remained closed, though I would have been surprised if he hadn't heard the ruckus of us fighting the ghoul. Evidently, he hadn't cared enough to intervene, and I was ninety-nine percent sure he would react the same way to our request for his help. All the same, what if the ghoul was still in the graveyard? Or if it came back—and brought friends? As much as I disliked the guy, he deserved to be warned that his house might end up surrounded by flesh-eating monsters. Unlike zombies, ghouls didn't rely on a summoner to give them directions. They were autonomous and far more dangerous.

"Hey!" I called to the Reaper and then rapped on the door with a muddy fist.

"Go away," said Harold.

"I'm doing you a favour," I returned. "I don't know if you heard us fighting it off, but there was a ghoul in your backyard."

The door nudged inward. "Didn't you get rid of it?"

"You knew it was a ghoul." *Of course he did.* "It'd have been nice if you'd enlightened us on what we might find. And even nicer if you'd come to help."

Harold scowled at us from the sliver of light in the doorway. "A lone ghoul shouldn't have been too much for the two of you to handle."

"We were expecting a zombie." I nodded to Perry, who picked more dirt out of her hair. "*Did* you know it was right behind your house?"

"No, of course I didn't."

I blinked. "Ghouls feed on the dead, don't they? Wouldn't you have expected it to pay a visit to the local graveyard?"

"I would have thought the beast would have stayed in hiding until the police had left the area." He gestured in the direction of the morgue. "Which I imagine was its plan before you two bumbling fools got in the way."

"Oi." I wiped my dirty palms on my equally muddy trousers. "The ghoul escaped, but it'll likely be back, and it might bring company."

"Not tonight." He made to close the door again, but I caught the wooden edge in my fingertips. "What do you want from me?"

"I want to know what that ghost told you," I said. "Ghouls are created when another ghoul bites a person. That means Elaine was attacked by one... but who turned *that* ghoul? Where'd it start?"

From my admittedly out-of-date Reaper lessons, I'd learned that ghouls passed on the virus through biting their victims, but there couldn't be *that* many in the area. Someone would have noticed.

Perry had gone pale beneath the muddy streaks on her face. "There might be any number of them. We need to find the nest."

"I imagine it won't be too hard for you to find," Harold growled. "I thought you Wardens knew what you were doing."

She met his stare evenly. "I thought you *Reapers* did too."

"If it comes back, you'll get rid of it, won't you?" I looked for his scythe, but he'd tucked it out of sight somewhere behind the door.

"If you people did your jobs, I wouldn't need to." Harold tugged the door out of my grip with a firm hand and closed it in our faces for the second time that night.

"Helpful." Perry blew out a breath. "I need to find my team and tell them."

"Good call." The rest of the Wardens ought to be able to shake together a plan for finding the ghouls' nest, but I didn't have much recollection of my Reaper lessons on the subject.

Perry and I left the cemetery through the gate and spied a huddle of figures standing outside the morgue.

"Perry!" Callum called over. "Are you all right?"

"No thanks to the ghoul." Perry overtook me and strode to join her team, all of whom stared in surprise at our muddy state.

"There was a ghoul?" Tam's eyes widened, bright green in the darkness. "Where?"

Perry pointed over the fence into the graveyard. "It's gone, but it'll be back when the coast is clear. I don't think it expected to come face to face with a Reaper, let alone two."

"Two?" Tam's gaze swung between me and the graveyard, comprehension dawning on his face. "The Reaper lives in there... The ghoul attacked him too?"

"No, it was hiding in the graveyard," I said. "Digging up the ground. The Reaper only knew it was there because a ghost warned him, but Perry and I ambushed the ghoul before it could launch a sneak attack."

"Did it plan to attack the Reaper?" Farley asked sceptically. "Ghouls aren't that smart, but you'd think it would have thought twice about picking a fight with him."

"No, I doubt it planned to target him," said Tam. "Most likely, it wanted to feed and then leave. *Why* the police didn't search the graveyard..."

"It's fast-moving enough to avoid attention. And sneaky." I opted not to mention it'd disarmed me. It was humiliating enough that old Harold thought the pair of us were incompetent. "I figured its nest must be nearby, but it left such a stench everywhere that I couldn't pick out the direction."

"I bet a shifter's senses can find it," added Perry. "Callum, want to volunteer?"

"To find a nest of ghouls at night?" The werewolf gave a shudder. "We don't even know how many there are."

"If all the other missing persons are in the same state, at least four." I suppressed a shudder too. "We also need to find out where this started. Ghouls are transformed by a virus, but the first one must have come from somewhere outside the town."

"Wait—are you saying the ghoul was the same person whose body disappeared from the morgue?" Callum's mouth dropped open as the truth dawned on him. "Elaine Langley?"

"Yeah, it turns out she isn't a zombie after all," I said. "Ghouls are far more annoying."

"You don't say," said a scathing voice.

All eyes turned to Maurice, who stood beside the rest of the team with his hood pulled up against the rain as if he'd never left.

"You." I glared at him. "Nice of you to show up. Want to help us find the ghouls' nest?"

"No, I don't think I will."

"Maurice," said Callum, "we don't have to find them tonight, but a nest of ghouls is a major problem."

"If you want to walk into a lair of monsters, leave me out of it," said Maurice.

"How do you know they're all hiding in one place?" asked Farley.

"They tend to group together," Tam said. "They also rally around the oldest of their number, the ghoul who initially bit the first victim."

"Rather like vampires," Perry added and received an ugly look from Maurice in return. "Just saying."

"We don't group together," the vampire retaliated. "Ghouls have a pack mentality that's more like animals than humans. If we find their nest, they'll swarm us. They're not going to wait nicely for us to corner them."

"With every person they turn, their numbers grow," Perry said. "We outnumber them, in all likelihood, especially when you add the two Reapers—but for how long?"

"One Reaper," I corrected. "Old Harold certainly won't come with us to a ghouls' nest."

"Won't he?" Maurice bared his teeth. "Or were you lying about his abilities?"

"He's a powerful Reaper, but he's also a lazy sod, not unlike someone else I could mention." I bared my teeth right back at him. "If we don't deal with the ghouls tonight, they'll have claimed another victim by morning. Are you sure you want that on your conscience?"

"Maurice isn't the one who decides for the rest of the team." Tam's warning tone caught the attention of the entire group, even me—despite my best efforts. "The nest might not even be within the town's boundaries, and it's dangerous for us to wander around at night without a clear plan."

"Didn't you see any signs of the ghouls' nest while you were out in the countryside?" I asked. "I thought you spent hours searching the river."

"We did, and we didn't see anything," Tam replied.

"Having said that, we didn't realise it was a ghoul that we ought to have been looking out for. The nest must be well hidden to have escaped our attention."

"Or inside Hawkwood Hollow itself." Not a pleasant thought. "I'm not kidding or trying to guilt-trip you, but if we wait until morning, someone else might get killed."

"We have too few clues to search for the nest tonight." Tam's voice held a hint of regret, but he spoke with a firm tone. "I'll inform the police. They can offer instructions to the public to avoid going outside until the nest is found."

"Then it'll be their own fault if they get bitten," added Maurice.

"Do you say the same to your own victims?" I didn't believe he'd played a part in any of this, but his attitude problem coupled with his convenient absence made me certain he would never have my back when I confronted the rest of the ghouls.

"Leave it alone, Maurice," Callum said wearily. "You're being obnoxious, and she's right. Someone might die if we don't act, but we have to make decisions as a team, and we need more information. Otherwise, we'd only be placing ourselves in danger unnecessarily."

"Precisely." Tam swivelled back towards the morgue. "I'll talk to the police myself… if you can refrain from fighting one another while I'm gone."

Perry made a quiet noise of irritation. "Dammit, I hate when he talks sense. We can't do this tonight."

"Not yet," added Farley. "Don't forget you scared the ghoul off. That might have discouraged it from biting anyone else."

I hope so. I wasn't foolish enough to take on a nest alone, not when I didn't know what else we might find. Someone had turned the first ghoul, after all, and there was no telling how far this stretched. It must go far beyond poor Elaine

Langley—not to mention the other missing persons, whose families would no doubt be waiting for answers. *Guess I should talk to the police too.*

Drew must still be in the morgue, so I followed Tam's path to look for him. Behind the officer standing outside, the morgue's gloomy interior looked even less appealing after the fight with the ghoul, but I could see Drew inside. I caught his eye and waved him over.

Drew approached the door, sidestepping the office guarding the way in. "Maura, why are you covered in mud?"

"We ran into a ghoul." I backed away from the morgue's entrance as he came over to join me, his concerned gaze taking in my bedraggled appearance. "Or Elaine Langley."

"You found her?" He looked up sharply, as if he'd expected to see her walking up the road when I spoke her name.

"She's not a zombie," I clarified. "A ghoul is a similar kind of creature, but it's rather more vicious, and faster. Unfortunately, it escaped, and we don't know where its nest is."

"What is going on out here?" Petra strode out of the morgue behind Drew, looking me over with disdain. "I do hope you weren't causing trouble in the graveyard, Reaper."

"Of course not," I said, annoyed. "I had a run-in with a ghoul. Turns out we aren't dealing with a zombie after all."

"You've changed your story?" She gave a haughty sniff. "I told you not to listen to her, Drew."

"I didn't change my story," I corrected. "I made an assumption based on past experience, but it turns out that Elaine Langley was transformed into a ghoul, not a zombie. I found out when she attacked us."

Perry, who'd been listening in, sidled towards us. "Yeah, a ghoul's transformation is quicker than a vampire's. That's why the body went missing."

"Really, now," Petra said. "Whereabouts is this creature now?"

"It escaped, but not before making a mess of the grave-yard." I pointed over the fence. "And disturbing the Reaper. If you don't believe me, you can ask him to confirm it was a ghoul."

"The Reaper knew, did he?" Disbelief dripped from her words like the rain trickling down her glasses. "How, exactly?"

"A ghost warned him." To Drew, I added, "I'm pretty sure the ghost was one of the other victims. He was young… a wizard, I think."

"A ghost?" He, unlike Petra, knew what that would mean. "Is he still around?"

"No… He moved on." He'd left me with a list of questions, including why he'd been calling to someone in the river and why he'd come to warn the Reaper. If it was Elaine he'd been trying to reach, did he know she was dead? Had he witnessed the attack on her? Not that we had any chance of asking him now that he'd gone, and Harold the Reaper would probably use his scythe on us if we disturbed him again.

"What are you talking about?" Petra demanded. "Is there a zombie, or isn't there?"

"There's no zombie, but there's something worse," I replied. "If one missing person turned into a ghoul, there's a fair chance the others met the same fate… and if we aren't careful, we'll have a whole swarm to contend with."

"How do we deal with them, then?" asked Drew.

I took a breath. "We need to find and destroy their nest."

9

A s much as I wanted to hunt down the ghouls right away, until we figured out where their lair might be hidden, we would only end up going in circles.

"I'll call you in the morning," Drew told me as I left the morgue along with the Wardens. "In the meantime, I can have another look into the details of the other disappearances to see where this might have started. Is it likely that the first ghoul came from outside Hawkwood Hollow?"

"I think so, but don't take my word for it on that." There were other possibilities, but I didn't have the focus to ponder them while I was drenched, covered in mud, and thoroughly exhausted.

With a mixture of relief and resignation, I joined the Wardens in heading back to the inn. The silence that pursued us down the dark street gave me a chance to consider the many questions the ghoul's attack had stirred up in my mind.

"If ghouls feed on dead bodies, where have they been getting them from?" Perry voiced one of my queries. "I mean, wouldn't that Reaper of yours have noticed them skulking around the cemetery before tonight?"

"Yes… he would have." It had only been a few days, but the ghouls must have found a feeding spot somewhere that wasn't in the local cemetery. Elaine, I was sure, had only been there because the police had found her body and taken it to the morgue, so the graveyard had been her nearest source of sustenance. *Ew.* "It's possible some of the missing persons were killed without being turned into ghouls… or they picked the lair of a serial killer as their hideout or something."

Perry pulled a face. "Delightful."

Farley made a noise of disgust. "Are serial killers common here?"

"No more than anywhere else." I decided against mentioning that the common factor in most criminal activity recently had been *me.* "You were out walking for hours. You really didn't see any places that might be hideouts for ghouls out in the countryside?"

"No, and I didn't pick up their stench, either." Callum wrinkled his nose. "That would have been hard to miss. I don't know, then."

"Don't forget that werewolf who chased you off," Perry reminded him. "We didn't search that field."

"Wait, you mean Tessa?" The estranged daughter of the pack chief preferred to live outside the town's boundaries, and she didn't take kindly to people trespassing near her house. "If I'd known you were going there, I'd have warned you she doesn't like visitors."

"Or clothes, either," Farley said wryly.

"That too," I added. "How close did you get to her house?"

"Close enough that she and Maurice almost got into a fight," Perry told me.

I raised a brow. "Who won?"

"Tam talked Maurice into stepping aside, so nobody did,"

Callum answered. "Ah—I assume she'd have reported anything suspicious to the police?"

"Yes, she would have." I glanced in the vampire's direction, only to find that he'd disappeared again. Either he'd decided to return to the inn by another route or he'd wandered off, but as it was typical for vampires to stay out all night and only return at dawn, I let it slide. Though it would've been nice if he'd promised to give the rest of the team a helping hand in looking for the ghouls' nest. "Maurice was wrong about there being another vampire in town. He must have seen a ghoul and assumed it was a vampire instead."

"Good point," said Perry. "Easy mistake to make, given how fast they move."

"That means there was a ghoul wandering the streets yesterday evening." Any unwitting humans who'd been out last night had had a lucky escape. "In the graveyard."

That begged the question of how the Reaper hadn't noticed, though the guy often didn't leave his house for weeks at a time, and he'd been none the wiser as to the ghouls' existence until the ghost tipped him off.

"Well, that's creepy," said Farley.

"The Reaper wouldn't have known about Elaine's body if not for the ghost warning him." Once again, I wished the ghost from the bridge hadn't disappeared before I had the chance to properly talk to him again… but he wasn't the only spirit in town. "Perry, do you know if I'd be able to summon Elaine's ghost even though she's walking around as a ghoul?"

"Good question." She pursed her lips. "She's dead, so it ought to be possible to summon her spirit, but I don't know how it works with ghouls."

"If they're like zombies, I should be able to summon her ghost. Both aren't in control of their bodies any longer." That meant it was entirely possible for a ghost to watch their own zombified corpse wandering around, as I'd discovered recently.

"Good idea." Perry dropped her voice and fell into step with me. "If you summon her ghost, I want in on it."

"Why?"

"Because she's a witness," she said. "To her own death."

"What're you two chatting about?" asked Farley.

"Ghosts," Perry replied.

"Figures," said Callum. "You two have a lot in common."

"I'm not sure if I should be flattered or insulted," said Perry. "I don't summon the dead *that* often. And I've never reaped anyone's soul."

"Hey, I don't even have a scythe," I protested. "Though old Harold generally uses his as a hat stand."

Farley's brow furrowed. "Is he not as dangerous as you told Maurice he was?"

"He is if you get on his bad side," I said. "A retired Reaper is still someone you don't want to cross. He *did* pick up his scythe after the ghost warned him there was a ghoul in his backyard."

"He didn't help you fight it off, did he?" asked Callum.

"He thought we could handle it ourselves." I felt myself flushing underneath the mud streaking my face. "He didn't know the Wardens were in town until he saw Perry."

"And he led us to believe it was a zombie." Perry sounded as if she felt put out by the ghoul's escape too. "We got taken by surprise in the darkness, but we won't make the same mistake again."

"Walking into the ghouls' nest at night is a worse mistake," Tam said. "They sleep during the day, so we might be better off hunting them down in the morning. They have the same sleep cycle as vampires do."

"Same attitude problem too," Perry added.

"Perry," Tam reprimanded, though the others laughed at

her comment, and since Maurice wasn't around to raise a fuss, the tension in the air dissipated a little. For the first time, I could see how Perry had become part of the team despite her obvious independent streak. She fit in with the Wardens the same way I fit in at the inn.

With the exception of the vampire, I did like Tam's team of misfits. Whether it was enough to trust them with my life, I didn't know yet, but finding the ghouls and stopping their murder rampage was a priority. And I didn't want to do it alone.

When we neared the inn, Tam addressed the rest of his team. "We'll start our search again in the morning. Deal?"

"Sure, but not first thing," said Perry. "Maura wants to see if Elaine's ghost stuck around before we head out."

"Ghosts can exist when their bodies are ghouls?" asked Callum.

"Zombies can, so we figured the same ought to apply to ghouls," I explained. "We're going to try to summon her and see how it goes. If we can get her story of the events that led to her being attacked and turned into a ghoul, we might be able to figure out where the others are hiding."

———

The next morning, I woke up bright and early, ready to summon a ghost. Or as ready as possible, anyway.

"You're wasting your time," Mart informed me as I left my room. "The ghost will flip out when she finds out her body is wandering around as a ghoul, if she answers you at all."

"Thanks for the encouragement." I'd woken up with a mild cold and a general sense of malaise, which I attributed to getting soaked to the skin yesterday. It was possible that some of Mart's current mood came from me monopolising the shower for an hour after I'd got back to the inn and using all the hot water.

He tailed me downstairs. "You *ditched* me last night."

"You said you didn't want to go to the morgue. Or the graveyard." Why a ghost would be afraid of places where dead bodies rested was a mystery to me, but he did have a point. If Elaine didn't already know her body was wandering around as a ghoul, she might not be too happy to find out.

I made a point of not summoning potentially dangerous ghosts inside the inn, so I knocked on Perry's door first. She answered, looking far more awake than I was, already dressed in a T-shirt and a pair of rain-splattered jogging trousers.

"Have you already been out?" I asked.

"Yeah, I like to go for a run every morning. Clears my head."

So much for us having a lot in common. "Weren't you worried you'd run into the ghoul?"

"Nah, they go back underground at dawn."

"Underground." Maybe that was where they were hiding… but whereabouts? "Okay, want to summon a ghost?"

"Absolutely."

Mart laughed. "You're *both* out of your minds."

"He woke up on the wrong side of the bed this morning," I said in response to Perry's raised eyebrows. "Metaphorically speaking."

He shot me another rude gesture and departed through the closed door to my room. Hoping he wouldn't flood the shower in protest at being left behind again, I walked downstairs with Perry.

We found a sleepy-looking Allie standing at the reception desk. "Morning, Maura. And… Perry. Are you going out?"

"Not for long." Guilt twinged inside me. She'd been waiting for me when I returned to the inn, and I'd explained our encounter with the ghoul to her and Jia. Carey, merci-fully, had gone to bed by that point, but I'd bet her mother had been up late worrying about the possibilities, though I'd reassured her there was little chance of the ghouls attacking the inn. Their aversion to running water would mean the odds of them crossing the river were next to none, and the only other routes to the inn involved climbing over walls and through bushes. Not impossible, but I didn't need to give anyone nightmares about ghouls slithering into their rooms.

My own imagination was overactive enough, and as Perry and I approached the river, I found myself scanning every shadow in case a ghoul was lurking out of sight in the bushes. We found nothing, of course, and safely reached the area that I'd got into the habit of using to summon ghosts out of sight of any onlookers. Perry wore a dubious expression as she took in the muddy patch of ground covered in the dispersed remnants of old summoning spells.

She watched me pull a small bag of herbs out of my pocket. "I thought Reapers could call the dead from anywhere without needing any props."

"We can, but I like to cover all my bases." I sprinkled the herbs in a circle in front of us and then stood back to face the empty space above. "Elaine Langley?"

Nothing happened. I'd expected as much, but I repeated her name a couple of times and then called on my Reaper powers. Perry's eyes widened as the darkness spread from my fingertips to the circle of herbs, opening a door into the afterworld.

"Elaine Langley?"

This time, light sparked on the other side, and a trans-parent figure appeared, hovering above the circle. Turning on the spot, the young woman pointed at me and let out a sudden shriek. "You!"

Well, that isn't promising. "Do I know you?"

"You're the Reaper!" she yelled. "Why didn't you stop them?"

"Stop who from doing what?" She'd lost me already, and the way her body was flickering around the edges warned me we didn't have much time before the afterworld swallowed her up for good. "Listen—do you remember how you died?"

"Obviously." She let out a huff. "Why didn't you stop them from finding my body?"

"Them?" *Huh?* "You mean the police?"

"Who else?"

"Why?" My mind blanked. "Didn't you want your family to know what happened to you?"

Perry sucked in a breath. "Ghouls can't cross running water. If her body had stayed in the river, it'd have slowed the transformation, if not stopped it outright."

"What?" I swivelled towards her and then back to the ghost. "That would have been helpful to know earlier. Also, I didn't have any idea there was a ghoul infestation until one attacked me last night. There's nothing I could have done."

"You should have done *something*," Elaine insisted. "You're the Reaper."

My confusion intensified. Spirits weren't usually this self-aware. "How did you know… Wait! You knew that guy, right? On the bridge?"

Her expression crumpled. "Alec tried to save me."

"He did?" Noting that the flickering around her body was intensifying, I skimmed my mental list of questions in search of the most urgent. "Your body transformed—do you know where it is now?"

"No." The ghost faded, and her cry rang out from the darkness shrouding her. "I don't want to go. Alec, help me!"

I lowered my hands as the shadows of the afterworld vanished along with the remnants of her scream.

Perry grimaced. "I bet being transformed into a ghoul made it hard for her ghost to stick around."

"Possibly." *Now what?* "I think that other ghost we saw must have been Alec… but what did she mean when she said he tried to save her?"

"Might he have tried to stop the ghoul from biting her?" She rubbed her forehead. "No, that doesn't work. Ghosts can't usually interact with anything living unless they're particularly strong, and I'm not sure that guy was."

"He knew her body was in the river." When the police had fished her out, they'd unintentionally sealed her fate, though she wouldn't have stayed in the water forever. Eventually, the transformation would have been completed. "That's how he knew she was turning into a ghoul…"

"Ghouls don't like running water, same as vampires," Perry said. "I wonder—did the ghost push her body *into* the river to stop the transformation?"

"He might have."

Speculating would do neither of us much good when there was nobody left to ask. Elaine and Alec were both dead, and their ghosts were gone. If their bodies had turned into ghouls, they would retain nothing of their former personalities.

As we turned away from the site of the summoning, I pulled out my phone and called Drew.

He picked up right away. "Hey, Maura. Are you okay?"

"Is the name Alec on the list of disappearances?"

"Let me check… Why?"

"It's the name of the ghost I saw at the cemetery yesterday," I said. "He and Elaine were friends, I think."

"Yes. Alec Delaney is the name of one of the victims. How'd you know?"

"I just spoke to Elaine's ghost."

"Maura." He sighed. "I thought I told you not to do anything rash overnight."

"If I hadn't summoned her ghost myself, Perry would have done it instead."

"The two of you seem to think alike."

"Everyone keeps saying that." I glanced up at Perry, who shot me a quizzical look. "Besides, Elaine's ghost wasn't able to stick around for long. Probably because her body is currently infected by a virus that turned her into a flesh-eating monster."

"Did she give you any clues about the location of the ghouls' nest?"

"She didn't have time to tell me before she vanished," I replied. "You might want to look into her friendship with Alec, though, and see if they interacted in the days before their deaths."

"Noted," he replied. "Can you try not to summon any more ghosts before then?"

"I won't. Don't worry. See you later."

When Perry and I returned to the restaurant, we found the Wardens occupying their usual table by the window. Allie was laying out breakfast on the buffet table at the back, and when I spied Carey, I remembered that I'd forgotten to come up with an excuse for running off at the end of the ghost tour. How much had Jia and Allie told her? Not about the ghoul, I assumed, but I braced myself for questions when I crossed the room to join her and her mother.

"Hey," I said to Carey. "Sorry I'm a bit late. I had to run an errand."

"Where'd you go last night?" Carey eyed the Wardens' table, where Perry had sat down with the others. "You were with them, weren't you?"

I weighed the options and went with the truth. "It turns

out the body the police found in the river yesterday was infected with a virus that turned it into a ghoul."

Her mouth dropped open. "Is there another monster in town? Is it coming here?"

"Ghouls don't attack living people, so we're safe here," I told her. "They're also scared of Reapers."

"Then why…?" The colour drained from her face, and her gaze snagged on Perry and the others. "They're Wardens, aren't they? Are they with the people who tried to shut us down?"

"No, they aren't," Allie reassured her. "They're from a different branch. They're here to help us."

Carey's mouth turned down at the corners. "Why didn't you tell me?"

"I didn't want to distract you from the tour yesterday," I said. "I also didn't know what we were dealing with until last night."

Her mouth flattened. "That's why you didn't want me to go outside alone, Mum, isn't it?"

As Allie opened her mouth to answer, the door opened, and several police officers walked into the room. I tensed, recognising Petra, though Drew was with them too. His expression was all business, though, and my heart lurched when Petra approached the Wardens' table.

"You're all wanted for questioning," Petra told them.

10

The Wardens' conversation paused as they took in the approaching police officers. Had Petra found out the information I'd passed on to Drew and decided it somehow implicated Perry and me in the deaths? If so, why would they come here now, when it was barely seven in the morning and nobody else was awake? To avoid witnesses?

Tam rose to his feet. "Is there a reason you want to talk to us?"

"We wish to discuss the events of last night," said Petra. "As we believe certain members of your group are withholding information."

"If you mean me, I told you everything." Perry cast a worried glance at me and then at Tam. Wait—Maurice wasn't here. Either the vampire had yet to return from his nighttime wanderings, or he was in his room at the inn, dead to the world. Pun intended.

"We'd appreciate your cooperation," said the officer. "If you'll come with us…"

"What's going on?" Carey whispered.

"Your guess is as good as mine," I whispered back, though I had some ideas. It wouldn't be the first time Petra had decided to obstruct me from helping in a police investigation, but why would she have decided to turn on the Wardens? I caught Drew's eye, but despite the flicker of annoyance in his expression, he was surrounded by other officers, and challenging them might backfire in his own face. "I'll see if Drew can help. Is that okay, Allie?"

"Of course." Allie watched the police lead the Wardens out of the restaurant. "Take as long as you need."

"I'll be back before my shift." *I hope.* I could just see Petra dragging this out for as long as possible, though she'd specifically asked the Wardens, not me, to come in to be questioned. Quickening my pace, I caught up to Drew at the doors. "What the hell is going on?"

"It wasn't my idea," he replied in an undertone. "You don't have to come."

"I'm not sitting this one out." I strode alongside him towards the bridge, where Petra had come to a halt.

"You seem to be missing a team member," she said to Tam.

"Maurice isn't at the inn," he told her. "He went out last night and hasn't come back yet. With your permission, I'll call him and let him know he's needed."

Her lips compressed. "Do that. The rest of you will come with us."

I had an inkling the sneaky vampire wouldn't be that easy to get hold of, and when we reached the other side of the river, Tam lowered his phone. "He's not answering, but I'll send him a message."

Petra didn't look overly happy at that, but even she had to admit she didn't have any hope of finding a vampire who didn't want to be found. The rest of the officers seemed to be following her lead, with the obvious exception of Drew, whom I assumed must have come along to stop her from going too far. Or to stop *me* from going too far. Either worked.

"There." Tam put away his phone. "He'll join us soon, I'm sure."

"I should hope so," Petra said. "The quicker you all comply, the quicker you'll be able to leave."

"I thought we had permission to look around for the creature we were sent to find," said Tam. "I showed you the paperwork."

"You *don't* have permission to interfere in an active police investigation, which you did by engaging with one of our missing persons."

"You mean the ghoul?" I spoke up out of sheer confusion. "We didn't know the ghoul was there until it attacked us."

"*Elaine* was a missing person whose tragic death was rendered even more tragic by the disappearance of her body."

"She was transformed into a monster," I pointed out. "What are you doing? Accusing the Wardens of stealing her body? Is that what you think?"

Petra's eyes narrowed at me. "You spoke to her ghost, Reaper. Didn't you?"

"So did I," Perry cut in. "Who told you that? Were you listening in the bushes?"

No... she must have heard Drew on the phone to me. Why did she want to talk to the Wardens and not me, though?

Petra's jaw twitched. "You banished her ghost without permission."

"We didn't banish her. She vanished of her own accord," I corrected. "I think the ghoul virus made it hard for her spirit to stay in the waking world, and I only had a brief time to talk to her. The same was true of Alec—and on that note, I'm pretty sure his body turned into a ghoul too. Did you hear that part of my conversation with Drew?"

Drew gave a faint groan, while Petra turned brick red. *She really was eavesdropping on us.*

"Enough," said Petra. "I won't hear any more stories from you, Reaper. It's frankly a pity that you lured the Wardens into breaking the law."

I choked on a laugh. "I didn't know summoning ghosts was illegal. I'll have to call the Reaper Council and let them know."

"You think this is funny?" Her eyes bulged. "There's a serial killer on the loose, and you find it amusing?"

"Who mentioned a serial killer?" My brief amusement faded. For her to be so vehement meant there must have been another development overnight... such as another disappearance.

Petra didn't reply, but when we reached the police station, she insisted on splitting up the Wardens to question them individually. She also sent a pair of officers to keep an eye out for Maurice's arrival, though I had my doubts he'd show his face. If the police were aware of the bite marks on Elaine's neck, he was the person most likely to be blamed, and I didn't know if Petra's new and inconvenient eavesdropping habit had extended to her listening to my previous conversations with Drew.

Admittedly, with Perry and me as the only witnesses, Petra might have simply convinced herself that the ghoul had never attacked us at all. While Harold was technically a witness as well, I didn't see him stepping forward to defend us.

"Great," I muttered to Drew as the Wardens disappeared into the interrogation rooms. "Why am I not on the suspect list, anyway?"

"They aren't suspects," he whispered back. "Petra is, ah, concerned that the Wardens aren't being entirely honest about their motives."

"You ought to reprimand her for listening in on your private phone calls."

"I should have taken the call outside of the office. It was my oversight."

I scowled. "She found out I summoned Elaine's ghost. How did she go from there to accusing all the Wardens of withholding information?"

"I'm not entirely sure, to be honest," he replied. "She doesn't like not being in control, and given the incident at the graveyard yesterday..."

"Should I have grabbed the ghoul and dragged it in front of her to prove it existed?" I dropped my voice in case Petra could hear us through the closed door to the questioning room. "Anyway, who was it?"

"Who was what?" Drew asked.

"The latest victim."

His brows shot up. "There isn't one... but someone else did disappear last night, shortly after we left the morgue."

Damn. Even if I hadn't been outvoted and the rest of the Wardens had opted to find the ghouls' nest last night, we might have been too late to save the person who'd been taken next. "A witch or wizard?"

"Wizard," he murmured. "And you're right... Alec Delaney was the last person to disappear before Elaine."

My throat went dry. "We have to stop this. Can you find a way to distract Petra while the Wardens and I search for the ghouls' nest?"

"Not until all the Wardens present themselves for questioning, and one is still missing."

I grimaced. "Maurice isn't going to show his face if he

thinks he's likely to get blamed for this. *Does* Petra know about the bite marks?"

Drew's mouth pressed into a thin line. "No, but when you mentioned the body walking away by itself, there's another creature that fits that description."

"Wonderful." I worked my jaw. "Petra's crossing a line."

"She's also very popular among the rest of the team," he said. "Especially those who believe I was wrong to involve a Reaper in police investigations."

"Oh, come on." I'd known I'd stirred up a lot of controversy, but this was ridiculous. I'd been trying to help. "What does she have against the Wardens? I thought she was all in favour of them arresting me."

"We can fix this if we act carefully," he said. "Do you and the Wardens have any idea where the ghouls' nest might be hidden?"

I shook my head. "I hoped Elaine's ghost would give us a clue, but no luck."

"I didn't know it was possible for someone to be a ghoul and a ghost at the same time."

"It's like with the zombies, remember?" I prompted. "Once they're dead, the connection between body and soul, spirit, whatever… it's severed. Her ghost wasn't able to stick around for long, but I'm not clear on the dynamic between Elaine and Alec. He died first, but his ghost stuck around to find hers. He must have known she was attacked next."

"Strange," he said. "I read the notes, and it looks like they were friends who spent a lot of time together, but you'd think he'd have wanted to warn her away from being bitten in the first place."

"Maybe his own ghoul-infected body hunted her down against his will." I shuddered. "Or she was with him when he died. No idea. We'll probably never know."

He was silent for a moment. "My fellow officers have never encountered a ghoul. Vampires are far more common."

"Ghouls have a few things in common with vampires," I said, "but once they transform, they become beasts with no memory of ever being human. They're definitely not the same."

"If the virus is spread by biting, where did it start?" he asked. "Do you think a ghoul came into the town from the outside?"

"Either that, or someone intentionally set one loose." I took in a breath, a distant memory of one of my long-ago Reaper lessons nudging its way to the surface. "Or…"

"Or what?"

"There's a second way to make a ghoul," I murmured. "It involves dark magic… and a ritual that's as likely to rebound upon the person using it as not."

"Did you say *ritual*?" He stiffened. "That sounds familiar, and not in a pleasant way."

"I know." I lowered my gaze to the floor, my skin crawling at the mere thought. "The thing with ghouls is that they're self-replicating. If someone wanted to flood a town with afterworld monsters, creating a single ghoul is the fastest way to do it."

We fell into a grim silence. Both of us knew someone who was all too willing to meddle in dark magic to get what she wanted, at any risk. If the ghouls had come from the same place as the last few incidents involving afterworld monsters, the odds of me being the intended target increased exponentially. But why pick ghouls? Despite their fast-replicating abilities, their dislike of running water would be a hindrance if they wanted to attack the inn… but the rest of town was another story.

Was I reading too much into this? Would even Mina Devlin go as far as to drown the rest of Hawkwood Hollow in ghouls to regain power, or was this a plot of someone else's devising? I didn't know, but it was all I could do not to hammer on the doors to the interrogation rooms and demand that Petra and her supporters stop wasting time before someone else got killed.

Tam emerged from questioning first. When he left the room, he and his interrogator exchanged a few calm words, which gave the impression that they'd been in an office meeting rather than an interrogation. Drew strode over to talk to the other officer, while I beckoned Tam to join me.

"Hey," I said to him. "What did they ask you?"

"Mostly what we were doing yesterday evening," he responded. "Why are you here? The police didn't ask you to come in."

"You didn't think I'd leave this alone, did you?" I glanced at the other rooms, wondering if he was half as patient as he pretended to be. "Perry and I are the only people who saw the ghoul last night, and I thought I might need to back up her story."

"True." His gaze went to the door leading to the room where Perry had been taken. Aside from Maurice, she was the person most likely to end up in trouble, depending on which officer was questioning her.

When Drew returned to my side, I cleared my throat. "Erm… who's questioning Perry?"

"Petra is."

I should have guessed. I swivelled back to Tam. "Where's that fanged friend of yours? If he wants to stand by the rest of his team, he ought to show his face."

"He will."

Am I imagining it, or does he not sound a hundred percent certain? I didn't trust the vampire, and evidently, Perry didn't either, but I'd thought the team leader had at least commanded Maurice's respect. Maybe the vampire had decided self-preservation won out over helping his team.

Callum emerged from his room next, which I'd expected. The laid-back werewolf wouldn't have tripped anyone's alarms, though worry clouded his face when he saw me and Tam standing alone with Drew.

"Perry and Farley aren't out yet?" he asked.

"No, and Maurice isn't here, either." Tam spoke in a low voice. "Can you have a look outside for him?"

"Of course." He made to walk away then hesitated. "Farley… she might want me to wait for her."

"True." Tam glanced at the closed doors to the remaining two interrogation rooms. "All right, I'll look for Maurice. You wait for Farley."

A look passed between the pair of them that I couldn't read. I was missing some context there, which was fine—they were entitled to their secrets—but I couldn't help wondering how Perry was getting on with being grilled by Petra. Or if Maurice intended to return at all.

When Tam walked out of the police station, I was left with Callum and Drew. Despite both being werewolves, they had absolutely nothing else in common. An awkward silence ensued until Drew looked at the clock on the wall and nudged me in the arm. "Maura, don't you have to be at work?"

I'd had the same thought. "I have half an hour. Besides, don't you think Allie and Carey would want me to tell them if any of our guests get arrested?"

"Nobody is getting arrested." He dropped his voice when another door opened and Farley walked out, her head bowed.

Callum strode to meet Farley and wrapped her in a hug. "Are you okay?"

She nodded tightly. "Yeah… Where are the others?"

"Tam's out looking for Maurice," he replied. "Perry's still being questioned."

"Oh." She took a step back, glancing at me. "She was the witness, right? Did she say anything about—"

"You don't have permission to discuss your private interviews with one another," said the officer who'd been talking to Farley. "You should wait outside, all of you. And you, Reaper... you aren't supposed to be here at all."

I didn't move. "I'm a witness too."

"She's here to help," Drew said to the officer. "She also has information on the incident at the cemetery last night."

"Yes. Perry wasn't the only person who saw the ghoul." I moved closer to the one remaining closed door and heard the murmur of conversation inside. "If Petra's unclear on the details, I can tell her."

Not that I *wanted* to talk to her, especially if she'd already made up her mind, but who else would?

"There's no need." The voice came from the other side of the door, and I jerked back when it opened and Petra herself emerged from the room. "Unless you have something to hide, Reaper."

I gaped at her, hoping she hadn't heard the rest of our conversation. "I thought there might be confusion on the details."

"Not at all." She stepped aside, revealing a bewildered-looking Perry behind her. "Go on."

Farley's shoulders relaxed when she saw her teammate. "Glad you're okay."

"We're all finished?" Perry directed her question at the officers as she left the room.

"Not quite," said Petra with a tight smile. "One member of your team is still missing."

"Tam's looking for him," Callum explained. "Ah—did you want us to stay here while we wait?"

"No, that won't be necessary." Petra retained that same inexplicable smile. "However, I would prefer for your team leader to consult the police before taking any more action on this investigation."

Dammit. What's she playing at? "Do you have a team ready to take down a nest of ghouls? Or would you rather wait for more bodies to pile up first?"

As Petra flushed, Drew stepped in. "Petra, we haven't discussed this. I don't believe it's necessary to restrain the other Wardens from proceeding with their mission."

"I'll be willing to reconsider the matter *after* I talk to their missing member," she said. "Better to be safe than sorry. Don't you agree?"

Drew's jaw tightened, but without Tam here to speak for the team, he had no way to argue in the Wardens' favour without looking as if he was supporting a group of outsiders over his fellow officers.

"You didn't answer the question," Perry said. "*Do* you have a team who are prepared to take on a nest of ghouls if you won't let us go looking for their nest?"

Petra gave her a withering look. "I'll thank you not to condescend to me, Miss Peregrine."

That was her full name? Perry shot me a brief warning look as if daring me to laugh before turning back to Petra. "That wasn't my intention. Several people have already been killed, and each person the ghouls bite will transform into another. If you aren't careful, you'll have an epidemic on your hands."

"Forgive me if I don't take your word for it," she said. "Until you or someone from your team bring me proof, I can't allow you to jeopardise our investigation. Now, I'll ask you to leave—and you too, Reaper."

My hands curled into fists. She was unrepentant. "I'll go, but if you see any signs of the ghoul, call me or call the Wardens. If not, your people are likely to come off worse."

Petra didn't answer, but she watched stony-faced as we left the building. Honestly, I didn't blame Maurice for keeping his distance. The question was, would the police find him before the ghoul struck again?

11

Despite how little I wanted to wait around for the ghouls to claim another victim, I returned to the inn since they weren't likely to emerge until the sun went down. I did my best not to act too distracted when Jia showed up and Carey went off to school, but it didn't help that the Wardens—minus Maurice and Tam—occupied the same table they had earlier. They sat huddled together, talking in low voices. None of the other patrons paid them much attention, though. Nobody else had been present when the police escorted them away, but their presence was distracting all the same.

"What're the odds that the vampire did a runner?" Jia watched their table from behind the bar. "What'll the police do if he turns out to have left town altogether?"

"Tam doesn't think he would, but I'm not sure the rest of the team agrees," I muttered back. "It depends if he thinks the police have decided Elaine was turned into a vampire and that they'll try to arrest him as a suspect."

"And by 'the police,' you mean Petra and her allies," said Jia. "Drew ought to smack her down if you ask me."

"She hasn't done anything wrong... at least on the surface," I said. "She claimed the Wardens were withholding information, and honestly, they might be, but I'd say she's more likely trying to find an excuse to stand in their way."

"What would she have to gain by that, though?" She began polishing a glass, an absent expression on her face. "She *wants* to stop those disappearances, surely."

"You'd think." Petra didn't believe a ghoul was responsible for the disappearances, and she wanted the police to solve this one alone... but she might be trying to discredit the Wardens because *I* had joined with them. She'd already put a fair bit of effort into trying to discredit Drew because of his unwavering support of me. "She's made it impossible for the Wardens to even try to find the ghouls' nest without telling the police their every move."

"Why would she want to sabotage her own investigation, though?" Jia put down the glass. "The police want to find the murderer, don't they?"

"She thinks it's a serial killer, not a paranormal monster," I said. "In her eyes, I'm a troublemaker, and so is Perry. And the Wardens are outsiders, besides. The police never set eyes on the ghoul, which gives us no proof to work with."

"What's Drew think of all this?"

"He's not impressed with her, obviously," I said. "But he can't do anything until she's finished talking to all the Wardens, so they'll be stuck at a stalemate until that vampire comes back."

"If he's a suspect, I don't really blame him for keeping his distance," she said. "Vampires are all about self-preservation."

"So much for him being a team player." I heaved a sigh. "I wish we'd managed to catch the ghoul and showed it to the police as proof. Or dragged in old Harold to back us up."

"Would he have been willing to talk to them?"

"Probably not, no." Disgruntled, I grabbed Jia's discarded

cloth and began scrubbing down the bar, more to have an outlet for my frustration than anything else. My annoyance mounted when Mart drifted past and knocked the cloth out of my hand.

"What was that for?" I turned to him. "Don't tell me you're still mad about me leaving you behind last night."

"You left me behind today as well," he said indignantly. "I could have eavesdropped on the interrogations."

"You were sulking in my room," I pointed out. "Besides, I doubt the police and the Wardens said anything we don't already know."

"If you're bored, you can go and talk to Perry," Jia suggested. "Or see if Tam has found the 'missing' vampire yet. It's not like the police can see you."

He made a rude noise. "If you want the vampire, find him yourself."

"Well, all right." I watched him float away through the bar. "Why's he so sensitive lately? I didn't think he'd be *that* bothered about being left out of a fight with a ghoul."

"No clue," Jia said. "Maybe he was worried about you yesterday."

"He has a hell of a weird way of showing it."

My brother glided across the restaurant and reached the Wardens' table, where he bowed. "Hello, my fine people. Can I get you anything to drink?"

I hastened over to the Wardens before one of them did take him up on his offer. "I wouldn't take the risk. He can sometimes levitate glasses without dropping them, but there's a one in three chance of you wearing it on your head."

"I'll take that under advisement," said Perry. "Were you talking about Maurice? Because we're thinking the same. If he doesn't show up soon, he'll be in a lot of trouble."

"I did wonder if Tam had found him yet," I said. "I'm guessing not, or else he'd have let you know. Unless… do you think he has a hunch that the police might have decided a vampire, not a ghoul, killed Elaine? What if Tam ends up having to choose whether to protect his teammate or send him to the authorities?"

There was an awkward silence during which none of the others looked at me. I'd touched on their own fears, no doubt, but they were the ones who had to make the final call. Or Tam did.

"I don't know," Perry finally said, "but we also have a job to do, and if Maurice doesn't show himself for questioning, we'll never get permission to carry on looking for the ghouls. That Petra woman has us cornered."

"Can't you—I don't know… contact your supervisors and ask them to talk to her?"

Not that I ought to encourage them, given that it had been the Wardens' supervisors who'd tried to have me arrested not so long ago, but who else would be able to override the police's authority? Certainly not me.

"Tam can call them," said Callum. "He might be doing that right now, in fact. But they're stretched thin and have bigger things to deal with than our argument with a local police department. They thought that if they sent five of us, we'd be able to handle the threat without too much of a struggle."

"Meaning the ghouls," I said. "They didn't know there'd be more than one, right? If it came down to it, would you be able to get rid of the ghouls' nest without a team member?"

"Sure," said Perry. "If we take them by surprise."

"You're joking," said Farley. "We don't even know where their nest *is*. Besides, we can't act without Tam's orders."

"Exactly," Callum said. "He'll have a plan. We just have to hold out until then."

Outvoted, Perry sat back in her seat and scowled. "I *hope* so. We only have until dusk before there's the risk the ghouls will claim another victim."

Exactly. I might have tried to convince Perry to ditch her teammates, but I didn't particularly want to break up their squad, and the police were as likely to hamstring me as the rest of them. Callum was the only member of the team who possessed enhanced senses, and I hadn't had so much as a whiff of the ghouls' foul stench since yesterday evening. Not enough to track down their lair.

Yet my acute awareness of the ticking clock made the morning drag even more than usual, and it wasn't until midday that I got a text from Drew. The message said, *I'm on my way. Don't go outside.*

My head snapped up, and Jia gave me a curious look. "What is it?"

"Drew warned me not to go outside." I stood on tiptoe, trying to see through the windows, but nothing seemed to be amiss in front of the inn. "He's on his way, apparently."

"Did something else happen?" she asked. "Another ghoul?"

"I thought they only came out at night." I could guess what *might* have happened, though. "Maybe Maurice got arrested."

Her nose wrinkled. "Why would he warn *you* not to leave the inn, though? He knows you and the vampire aren't friends."

"He might want to avoid them figuring it out." My gaze went to the Wardens, but none of them showed any signs of having heard. They hadn't received any ominous messages from their leader, presumably.

Another possibility was that the police had already found a clue as to the ghouls' location and decided to act alone. If they went looking for the monsters without the Wardens or a Reaper, it might end in disaster, but Drew wouldn't let them take the risk—would he?

When Drew showed up at the inn, the Wardens watched him enter with mild curiosity but didn't leave their table.

I strode out to meet him. "What's going on?"

"Petra's team found the body," he said. "That is—the body of the missing wizard from this morning. Otto Prendergast."

My heart lurched. "He hasn't transformed?"

"Yet," he said grimly. "Unfortunately, he had the same marks on his neck as the other victims, and this time, the damage was more extensive."

"The rest of the police know." Or Petra did, which made the vampire's absence look even more suspicious.

"Exactly."

"Where's Tam?" I glanced over at the Wardens' table. "He was looking for Maurice…"

"I don't know, but wherever that vampire is, he hasn't shown his face to the police yet," Drew said. "Needless to say, Petra has drawn her own conclusions."

"He wasn't even in town at the time of the first disappearance." I swore under my breath. "Where'd they find the body?"

"In an alleyway," he replied. "Too close to the high street for my liking."

"Is that why you told me not to go outside?"

"No, I just wanted to make sure you didn't run into the vampire by accident," he explained. "With the way Petra's behaving, it wouldn't surprise me if she had anyone associating with a suspect dragged into the station for suspicious behaviour."

"She wants me gone." It didn't entirely surprise me that she'd gone to such lengths to discredit me, but what did she have to gain by obstructing the Wardens as well? "If she keeps this up, someone else is going to get killed."

His jaw twitched in annoyance. "I told her not to act hastily, but it's hard for anyone who doesn't know better not to put two and two together about the vampire's disappearance and the body turning up."

"Figures." I swivelled towards the table where Perry sat with the others. "Want to tell them?"

"They'll find out soon enough, I don't doubt." He walked with me to their table, where Perry rose to her feet.

"What is it?" she asked. "Did they find Maurice?"

"No, but they found the body of the last victim—Otto Prendergast," I explained. "He hasn't transformed yet, but the police think he was bitten by a vampire, not a ghoul."

"Seriously?" She sank back into her seat. "Don't they have someone on staff who knows how to recognise an actual vampire bite when they see it?"

"The body will be examined," said Drew, "but unfortunately, certain members of the team see the marks as proof of your teammate's guilt."

Callum swore. "No way. A ghoul's bite marks don't look anything like a vampire's."

"Does Tam have a picture of both?" I asked. "In the Wardens' records?"

"Of course he does, but does that mean a certain trigger-happy officer will actually look at it?" Perry enquired.

"I will," Drew said. "I'm still the acting authority, but the body is currently ensconced in the morgue, and it won't be fully examined until later. When will the transformation start?"

"Tonight, I assume." I looked to the others for confirmation. "Would putting it in a freezer stop the transformation? Or slow it down?"

"Nope," said Perry. "It'll just make for a very cold and angry ghoul."

"Wonderful." I shuddered. "Great. I suppose we could just wait it out, but then we'll have five ghouls wandering around town, looking for victims. If not more."

"Is there a way to stop the transformation?" Drew asked.

"Destroy the body," Perry answered promptly. "I'm guessing that won't be a popular idea?"

"Definitely not," said Drew. "If Otto were a vampire, it'd technically be murder to destroy the body mid-transformation. No doubt Petra has familiarised herself with that law."

"I never thought about the technicalities of vampire law before," I remarked. "Petra's hardly an expert, though. If we *did* have a local vampire or two, we'd have more people who can tell the difference between their bites and those belonging to other monsters."

"People who aren't us," added Perry. "That's the crux of the problem, isn't it? That Petra has something against the Wardens."

"She was willing to support the ones who tried to have me arrested." I lowered my voice, conscious that we weren't alone in here, though the lull before the lunchtime rush meant the restaurant was fairly quiet. "I'm the one she has an axe to grind with."

"She's angry." Farley's hands clenched on the table. "It's hard to be around someone so… volatile. Is it all directed at you?"

"No, of course not," said Drew. "She wants the killer to be found, too, but we disagree on methods."

"And on whether there's a serial killer at all," I added. "Also, does a vampire biting people even count as a serial killer? Usually, their victims aren't dead. Not in the usual way."

"Beats me," said Perry. "We can recognise monster bites, but don't ask us about the magical laws governing those monsters."

"Vampires are a niche area," said Drew. "That said, there seems little point in spending the day looking up the laws when the ghoul's transformation this evening will speak for itself."

"Except if you're Maurice," added Callum. "He's in a bind, make no mistake."

Yeah. But does he want to take the other Wardens down with him? And what about Tam? Did he expect to find the vampire, or was he looking for the ghouls' hideout under the guise of searching for his missing teammate? That was what I'd have done in his place, but the guy struck me as someone who'd never had to deal with the law backfiring on him before.

At least I didn't have a ghost tour to plan for the evening, though it might have been a decent distraction from waiting for more news. After Drew left, I returned to helping Jia with the lunchtime rush and doing my best to ignore the Wardens' increasing impatience and Mart's continued sulking in the background.

In the middle of the afternoon, Perry and the others left the inn to "get some air."

"Or to find their leader," Jia remarked. "I find it hard to believe he's been looking for the vampire the whole time."

"That's what I was thinking," I said. "If I were him, I'd have seized on the chance to find the ghouls' hideout while the police are distracted."

"Is that what Maurice is doing, do you think?"

"No way," I said. "He made it clear that he thinks it's foolish for anyone to hunt down the ghouls alone, even during the day."

"If Tam's with him, he'll have backup."

"Hmm." I had my doubts that the prickly vampire would want to risk his own neck. "I can't figure out where the ghouls are hiding. If they're in the middle of town, it'd be hard for the Wardens to track them down without the police standing in their way, but they'll run out of patience at some point."

"So will you," she said. "I know you're itching to join them."

"The Wardens at least have a permit." I ground my teeth. "Not that it did them much good in the end."

I wished I'd got Perry's number or one of the others', but the only message I received that afternoon was a repeated warning from Drew telling me not to leave the inn. Taking that to mean Petra's team was still walking around, making nuisances of themselves, I stayed put until Carey came home from school.

Carey wasted no time in bombarding me and Jia with questions about this morning's incident, and since I had no energy left to hold back, I told her everything.

"There's a monster in the morgue *now?*" she asked. "And the police don't have any idea?"

"They think he's going to turn into a vampire," Jia explained. "They don't believe the ghouls exist."

"Drew believes me," I added, "but since there's no evidence, he's not going to be able to convince the others until the ghoul actually transforms."

"That's ridiculous," she said indignantly. "What about the Wardens? They're not allowed to get involved?"

"Not until they've all been cleared by the police," I said. "And even if Maurice does show up and let them interrogate him, there's no guarantee they'll give the rest of the team permission to act. Not if they've decided he's guilty."

"We have to stop them!" Carey said. "You're going to help, right, Maura?"

I looked at my phone, biting my lip. "Of course I am, but my hands are tied. If I knew where the ghouls were hiding, I'd be able to hunt them down alongside the Wardens, but we don't."

Where are *they hiding?* A town of this size only had so many hiding places, or so one would think, but I knew from experience that it wasn't that simple. Hawkwood Hollow's history—meaning the floods—had left all kinds of hideouts for potential nefarious activity, including abandoned houses, even whole streets that had been left to rot.

My thoughts drifted back to the river itself. Ghouls couldn't cross running water. They couldn't be that close to the town's main water source, however much they liked the cold and damp. *Right?*

"You should be able to," Carey said, yanking my attention back to the present. "What about old Harold? He's a Reaper, so he can fight the ghoul, can't he?"

"Oh, *he's* not going to exert himself," I said. "He said the Wardens ought to be able to handle this themselves."

"He didn't know they were here?" She gave a pause. "Who called them to come to Hawkwood Hollow, if not him? Or the police?"

"That's what I've been wondering." Unfortunately, my evidence for *that* was even less substantial than my proof that a ghoul, not a vampire, was responsible for the disappearances. "I have a feeling that certain people would be more inclined to accept the Wardens' help if they hadn't teamed up with me."

Jia gave a low whistle. "If you're right, someone *really* has it in for you."

"That's nothing new." Hell, the ghouls might have been intended to target me as well. I'd need to find their source to figure that one out, and the first ghoul had to have come from somewhere outside… but that was a question we'd be unlikely to find the answers to even if we tracked down the ghouls' lair. They couldn't speak, and their ghosts were gone. The newest was the only exception, and it was too early to contact him.

With the dead beyond reach, I was hard-pressed to figure out how to use my Reaper powers to solve this one.

12

As evening arrived, the inn started to feel more and more oppressive. It didn't help that it was raining again, curtains of drizzle cloaking the windows and pattering on the roof. I went outside a couple of times to check if the Wardens were around, but there was no sign of them.

"You'd think even the ghouls would avoid going out in this weather," Jia remarked to me as we cleaned the restaurant at the end of our shift.

"They like the cold and damp," I replied. "Swimming, not so much."

Drew had messaged me, saying he intended to take a team to watch the morgue that evening in case of another escapee incident, but that had been a couple of hours ago, and I hadn't heard from him since. With the lack of any ghost tours tonight, it was no wonder the inn was quiet. The few guests aside from the Wardens had gone back to their rooms.

Carey stayed put, helping us to clean the restaurant, though I knew the missing guests were on her mind as well. After Jia had gone home, Carey suggested watching a movie.

"The ghosts would like that, wouldn't they?" She indicated the games room. "We can watch it in there."

"I guess." Mart was still in a mood with me, and not even my attempts to bribe him with free showers had got through to him. "All right, go ahead. I'll finish cleaning up in here."

While Carey went in to set up the movie night, I went looking for my brother and found him lurking in the kitchen.

"What's the issue?" I asked. "You don't want to come with me to hunt the ghouls, do you? I thought you hated them."

"It would be *nice* to have a little consideration," he said. "And not to be taken for granted."

"When have I ever taken you for granted?" I asked. "You do whatever you like."

"Since our new guests showed up, of course."

"Are you jealous of them?" I stifled a laugh. "I'd have thought you'd be happy that more than one person can see you."

He scoffed. "I followed that vampire everywhere for you, and you didn't offer a word of thanks."

"I didn't?" I thought back. "Sorry."

"Not good enough."

"What do you want, me to throw myself down at your feet and beg for your forgiveness?" I shook my head at him. "I'll make it up to you later, but we have a nest of ghouls loose in town, and the authorities are being as much use as a chocolate teapot. Can you blame me for being a little distracted?"

A scream rang out from the lobby. My head jerked up. *Allie.*

I ran across the restaurant and through the doors before skidding to a halt at the reception. Allie crouched behind the desk, while a ghoul loomed over her. My mouth dropped open as disbelief froze me for a moment—then instinct kicked in.

"Hey!" I shouted, and the ghoul swung towards me.

I fumbled for my wand as the monster slither-crawled across the lobby floor, causing the automatic doors to the restaurant to slide open. At least nobody was inside, but I couldn't believe a ghoul had got into the inn.

How did it cross the river? Questions exploded in my head, but Carey's gasp from behind me when she saw her mother brought me back to reality.

The Wardens weren't around to help. There was only me.

Shadows flooded my palms, and the ghoul recoiled through the open door into the restaurant, leaving a trail of dampness across the floor I'd spent an hour mopping earlier. I gave chase, pointing my wand at the monster.

My first freeze-frame spell missed when the ghoul slithered underneath a table. My second hit the table instead, causing it to fly into the air and then hover there as if held up by an invisible pair of hands.

Hearing movement behind me, I turned to see Carey watching open-mouthed from the doorway to the games room. "What *is* that?"

"A ghoul." I held up my free hand. "Go with your mother and hide. I'll deal with this."

The afterworld answered me, shadowy magic sweeping around my palm, but the ghoul slithered away from my advancing path.

"Get back here."

The ghoul had left a damp trail in its wake, causing my feet to slip, and I had to grab the table for balance as it dove behind the bar. I didn't want to destroy Allie's property if I could help it, so I approached the bar cautiously, hoping to sneak up on the monster. To my consternation, the beast rose upright and vaulted over the bar, leaving slime all over the polished surface in the process. *Oh, come on.*

"Hey!" I veered out from behind the bar and fired off a spell, which knocked over a table instead of hitting its target. The ghoul was too damn fast.

Then again, so am I. Shadows folded around my feet, and I leapt through, intending to land on top of the ghoul. Instead, my knees collided with a table, and my arms closed around thin air. I swore explosively when I landed in a crouch that further jarred my legs. *Where the hell did it go?*

I lifted my head in search of my target and saw that the ghoul had climbed up the wall, its claw-like hands digging holes into the plaster. *I didn't know they could climb.*

My knees throbbed as I straightened upright. From here, I could see the ghoul was dressed in the same jacket and jeans as the one that had attacked us at the cemetery yesterday. It wasn't the recent victim, but Elaine had come back for a second round. *Why? More to the point—how?*

As I stared in shock, the doors slid open, and Tam came charging in, the rest of his team fast on his heels.

"Where—" Perry's eyes bulged when she saw the ghoul clinging to the wall. "I didn't know they could climb."

"Neither did I." I stepped back, my knees screaming discontentment at their collision with the table. "It's fast."

"We'll corner it," Tam told the other members of his team. "Callum, take the other door. I'll stay here. Perry and Farley—"

"Wands out," they both finished in unison, suggesting they'd used a similar strategy before.

Tam blocked the front exit, while Callum moved in front of the door connecting the restaurant to the lobby. Perry and Farley, meanwhile, lifted their wands. I did the same, but the ghoul shimmied out of our reach, its claws raking holes in the wallpaper.

"Watch out," I warned. "Please try not to cause any property damage, won't you?"

All three of us took aim, and our spells crashed into the wall one after another. The ghoul had clawed its way to the ceiling before a spell finally hit its mark. With a high-pitched whine, the ghoul dropped from above like a falling rock.

The instant it landed, Callum shifted into a large wolf and rugby tackled the ghoul, pinning it down.

"Now!" Tam shouted.

Perry and Farley pointed their wands at the ghoul, and twin streams of fiery light erupted from the ends. Callum released the ghoul as flames engulfed its ragged body, and seconds later, nothing but dust remained.

"What the hell was that?" I stared at the spot the ghoul had occupied, my heart racing. "What did you do that for?"

"Huh?" Perry lowered her wand, confusion furrowing her brow. "We got rid of the ghoul."

"You got rid of the *evidence*." I pressed a hand to my forehead, adrenaline continuing to pulse through my nerves. "Couldn't you have done literally anything else? Frozen the ghoul? Turned it into a statue?"

"You're welcome?" Perry said. "Better to destroy it than let it bite someone else. Including you."

"Reapers are immune." I hobbled over to the spot where the ghoul had landed, my knees still throbbing. "Not that I'm not grateful for your help, but how are we supposed to figure out where it came from without a trail? It was the same one from the graveyard yesterday."

"Was it?" Perry's gaze shadowed. "Wait—how did it get over the river?"

"I was wondering the same thing," I said. "And just where is that vampire friend of yours? Has he shown himself to the police yet?"

The awkward silence that ensued spoke for itself. At the

doors, I spied both Carey and Allie peering in from the restaurant, checking the coast was clear, no doubt.

Allie caught my eye. "Is it gone?"

"It is," I said. "Sorry about the floor."

"I'm just glad nobody was hurt." She entered the restaurant, followed by a trembling Carey. "We can easily clean up."

"I'll do it." I gave the Wardens a pointed look. "Unless any of you want to lend a hand?"

Callum, still in his werewolf form, gave me a look that I'd have described as "sheepish" if it hadn't been on a giant wolf, while Farley and Perry lifted their wands to help me return the tables to their former places.

When I'd finished putting everything back where it belonged, Carey whispered, "Did someone send that monster after you, Maura?"

"If they did, they didn't plan well." I lifted my wand to clean the mud the ghoul had left on the ceiling and wall, but the gouges its claws had made in the plaster would be trickier to repair. "Ghouls are scared of Reapers, and once it realised I was here, it went on the defensive."

"It might have been after us instead," Perry commented. "How'd it get over the river, though?"

I waved my wand, causing a streak of mud to vanish. "The last time I saw it was in the graveyard, so it's anyone's guess."

"This was the same ghoul as the one you ran into yesterday?" Tam asked. "The one that attacked you?"

I inclined my head. Mart had disappeared after our spat earlier, but I spotted him lurking behind the bar when I went over to clean up the trail of muddy water the ghoul had left on the surface.

"The newest victim hasn't turned into a ghoul yet," said Perry. "Or if he has, we haven't heard."

"Where in the world have you all been for the past few

hours?" I tried to keep my voice calm, but Farley took a step back all the same. "Not helping the police, I assume."

"Actually, yes," Tam said. "To the best of our abilities."

"Did Petra appreciate that?" I already knew what the answer would be. "I'm surprised she didn't tell you to go away."

"She didn't," said Perry. "Tam was the only one of us who actually spoke to the police. The rest of us kept tabs on the ghoul and hunted for their nest."

"Oh." Knowing that they'd been trying to find the ghouls the whole time made me feel less like the day had been a waste, but evidently, they hadn't succeeded. "Did you find any clues as to its location?"

"Not until now." Tam indicated the spot where the ghoul had disappeared. "We were on our way back when we saw the ghoul disappear into the inn."

"You didn't see where it came from?"

"No," said Farley. "It seemed to come out of nowhere."

A laugh rang through the air. "That's one way of putting it."

All eyes swung towards the door, where Maurice stood. He was dripping wet, as was to be expected of someone who'd been out in the rain all day, and from the expressions on the others' faces, they hadn't expected to see him any more than I had.

Even Tam raised his brows at the vampire. "There you are."

"You did come back," said Perry.

"Well observed," said Maurice sardonically. "How did it take five of you to deal with a single ghoul?"

"You knew?" I narrowed my eyes at him. "Just where have you been hiding? Would you have cared if your team got into trouble because of you?"

"What do you know?" Tam cut in, his tone urgent. "This is important. The ghoul—how did it get to the inn?"

The vampire's jaw worked as if he were debating holding his tongue out of sheer stubbornness. Then he spoke. "There's a tunnel underneath the river. I think the ghouls' nest must be somewhere down there, but I didn't go all the way in."

"There's a tunnel… under the river?" *No way.* "How close to the inn?"

"Right there, by the bridge."

I made a sceptical noise. "Ghouls don't like crossing running water. What kind of place is that for them to choose to make their nest in?"

"Don't ask me," said Maurice. "It's a convenient spot if someone wanted to overrun the inn with ghouls."

"Like I said, Reapers are immune." The others, including Allie and Carey, weren't, but if anything, I had a dozen more questions than I had previously. "They're not the most obvious choice of creatures to use against me."

Except for their annoying ability to multiply—not to mention to avoid being caught—they had few advantages compared to similar afterworld monsters. *Has Otto transformed yet? Or are the police still waiting at the morgue?* Whether or not Maurice knew *that* was debatable, if he'd been hiding underground, but he would have only needed to delve into the thoughts of one of the officers to figure it out.

Another suspicion hit me. "How long have you known about the tunnel? Is it how you got back to the inn before?"

If so, he'd known about a potential route the enemy could use long before anyone else, including the rest of his team.

Maurice's mouth parted. "No, I haven't used the tunnel myself. I also didn't know you had no idea it was there."

I didn't know whether to believe him. How could nobody have noticed a tunnel right near the river? Yes, it had been dark and rainy all week, and most people had avoided going outside…

"You're free not to believe me," he added, "but the tunnel entrance is near the inn, and it's dark."

That meant the ghouls were ready to come out and feed. A shudder ran through my body. As strange as their choice of lair might be, the river was certainly an ideal spot for creatures that fed on the dead.

"The latest ghoul will be ready to join them soon," Perry murmured. "That ghoul is more likely to attack someone than the others are, since it'll have to walk out in the open and cross the town to reach the nest."

"The others aren't lying low either, considering one of them came here." I turned to the vampire. "Unless it left its hideout because it heard an intruder?"

I knew he'd taken a risk in coming back to the inn, but my mind was reeling. The existence of a tunnel near the river conjured up all sorts of implications that I didn't have time to consider, most of which were connected to the flood that had claimed the life of the Reaper's apprentice and caused the town to end up overrun with ghosts in the first place.

Maurice glowered at me. "I came back to warn you. I won't bother next time."

And with impeccable timing, Petra walked in through the front doors, a smug smile on her face. "I knew you were hiding that vampire somewhere. Arrest him at once."

13

When Petra gave the order, several other police officers entered the restaurant. Drew wasn't with them, and I had the sinking suspicion that Petra hadn't asked permission before "borrowing" several of his officers to come here.

"Well?" Petra asked the Wardens. "What do you have to say for yourselves?"

"Do we look like we've been harbouring a fugitive?" I gestured to the muddy floor, wishing I'd left the tables upended to add credence to my story and wishing even more that the Wardens hadn't decided to disintegrate our target. "A ghoul attacked us. Maurice came back to help his team."

I'd give him credit for that. If he'd shown up sooner, though, we might have avoided a confrontation. Unfortunately, I was willing to bet that Petra had been waiting for this opportunity.

"Actually," she said, "it does look as if you've been hiding a fugitive."

"Did you not hear what he just said?" I asked. "Maurice

said himself that he came back to warn us. He wouldn't have said that if he'd been here all along, would he?"

The vampire shot me an ugly look that was entirely deserved, but I didn't see any point in pretending we'd become BFFs. That would only make Petra and her allies more inclined to disbelieve us than they already were, and while I didn't particularly want to get the whole team arrested, it was better than Allie getting into trouble for something that had nothing to do with her.

Petra ignored me. "I told you to arrest him."

Two officers closed in, and Maurice tensed, his gaze darting towards the nearest exit. My heart plummeted, dread gripping me. If he ran, they'd never catch him, and everyone —including Petra—knew it. They would, however, have an ironclad reason to label him as the main suspect and dismiss all other options.

Time seemed to stretch out as the vampire lifted his head and caught Tam's eye. Tam shook his head slowly. At that, Maurice stilled, not moving an inch while the officers put handcuffs on him. His voice rang with tension when he spoke. "Why am I being arrested, exactly?"

"I'd like to know that myself," said a new voice.

All eyes turned to the door, which slid open as Drew entered. Momentary confusion crossed his face when he saw Callum, in the form of a wolf, sitting on the muddy floor. Then anger tightened his expression as he took in the sight of Maurice handcuffed in front of Petra and her fellow officers.

"I thought it was self-explanatory," said Petra. "This vampire refused to come to be questioned when he was invited to speak to us earlier, and you yourself found evidence that a vampire was responsible for murdering Otto Prendergast. Naturally, when I saw him in here, I had to take immediate action."

"I beg to differ," said Drew. "I never said the bite marks on the body belonged to a vampire. If you would allow an expert to look, they'd be able to tell the difference."

"Who exactly?" She gestured towards Perry and the others. "Surely not these individuals? It's plain to see that they've been supporting their fugitive teammate and cannot be trusted."

Tam stepped forward. "None of us knew where Maurice was until he showed up here. That's the truth. If you want to question him, you're welcome to, but we don't need to examine the body to prove that Otto was bitten by a ghoul. The transformation will start within the next few hours."

"You might want to make sure none of your people are standing in the way when it does," I added to Petra. "Those ghouls move fast. Oh, and it turns out they can climb walls too."

Petra gestured to her officers as if I hadn't spoken. "Take him away. If he tries to escape, you know what to do."

What does that *mean? Does she have some kind of contingency plan for dealing with a vampire?* Whether she did or not, I didn't want to prolong any conversation with her when Drew was the one who needed to be warned about the ghoul nest's location. Not Petra. No way did I want *her* in charge of investigating the tunnel Maurice had warned us about.

I held my tongue until Petra followed the officers out of the inn. Then I hobbled over to Drew, who asked, "Why are you limping?"

"We were just attacked by another ghoul—which the Wardens destroyed using a spell," I told him. "According to Maurice, the ghoul reached the inn through a tunnel underneath the bridge."

"What?" He spun towards the door, but I caught his arm before he followed Petra.

"Wait for the others to leave first," I warned. "They'll only get in our way."

"They arrested an innocent man."

"I know, but the tunnel must be well hidden to have avoided attention until now." I couldn't see how nobody else had stumbled upon it in the past two decades, but that was a question for later. As Tam made to follow Petra out of the inn, I called to him. "Wait—are you going after the ghouls' nest?"

"No, I'm going to the police station," he replied. "To make sure that Petra doesn't try to arrest Maurice for an unjust cause."

Right. He and the others would, understandably, want to prioritise their teammate. Who knew, maybe the ghoul would transform while they were there and prove the vampire wasn't responsible for Otto's death—but what about the other ghouls? If someone had set the first upon the inn, the others would follow. The Wardens didn't know about the enemies I'd made, though, and I didn't have time to fill them in.

Farley glanced over at me and then addressed her team leader. "Ah, don't you want to wait for Callum to shift back into human form before you go out again?"

The werewolf growled. He'd landed on top of his clothes when he shifted, but he would still be stark naked when he turned back into a human. While werewolves didn't generally have much need for modesty, there *were* a lot of people in the room.

Tam halted in the doorway. "I'll give you all five minutes to get ready. We can't spare much longer than that."

"Wise idea if there are more ghouls scuttling around outside." Perry crossed to the lobby, the werewolf trailing behind her and Farley bringing up the rear.

I made to follow, but my knees reminded me of the recent injury by screaming at me. "Ow. Bloody ghoul."

"The table did more damage to you than the ghoul did." Mart snickered.

"Thanks for the input. That was for my brother, not you," I added to Drew. "I crashed into a table when I was chasing the ghoul. It wasn't my finest moment."

I waved my wand, casting a pain-relief spell on my knees. It'd wear off in a few hours, but if I had to face more ghouls that night, I needed to be in top form.

Drew watched me with concern. "Which ghoul? Not Otto?"

"No, it was Elaine from yesterday. I recognised her clothes," I said. "That's why I'm inclined to believe Maurice. If the ghouls have a nest under the river, it explains how they've evaded attention, but it looks like they're on the move."

"You want to go after the ghouls' nest now?" he asked. "And destroy it?"

"Better than waiting for the others to show up at the inn."

"Why, though?" he asked. "I don't get it. Even if there *is* a tunnel under the river, I thought ghouls weren't that intelligent. Why would they choose to come to the inn rather than looking for victims closer to their nest?"

"I have a feeling someone gave it orders," I said quietly. "Probably the same someone who created the first ghoul."

"Created?" Perry stepped into view. Apparently, she hadn't followed her teammates upstairs after all. "You think someone—a *human*—sent that ghoul after you?"

A moment passed while I weighed up the pros and cons of telling her the truth. Out of everyone on her team, Perry was more likely both to believe me and to understand why finding the nest took priority over stopping the police from arresting Maurice… but that didn't make for any guarantees.

Ah, screw it. "There's a powerful witch who has a grudge against me, and she's been known to have worked with people who dabble in necromancy. This scheme has her fingerprints all over it too."

Perry's brow furrowed. "Why? Sending a ghoul after someone seems a bit excessive."

"I got her kicked out of town for covering up murders. It's kind of a long story."

"But… why would she target the inn?" Her gaze went to Allie and Carey, who were engaged in a whispered conversation near the bar. "Seems a bit harsh to go after your employers too."

"She's nasty and unscrupulous—and so are her supporters," I said. "This isn't the first time she's used afterworld monsters to target my friends. In fact, I'd wonder if she was the one who called the Wardens if not for…"

If not for another suspicion I had, but I needed to discuss that one with Drew first.

"Perry, are you coming?" Callum returned, back in his human form and fully dressed, and behind him walked Farley and Tam.

Perry hesitated. "Does Maurice really want me to be there while the police interrogate him?"

"We're sticking together," Tam said firmly. "That's the best way to avoid any more trouble."

"Is it, though?" Perry asked. "A ghoul attacked the inn. If Maurice is right and the nest is by the river, there'll be others. Are you sure you want to leave Maura to fight them off alone?"

"I thought there was a second Reaper," said Callum.

"He's on the other side of town and won't lift a finger to help me," I told them.

Farley made a noise that might have meant "I can't imagine why." That was fair enough, given that I hadn't exerted much of an effort to help Maurice escape custody, but the vampire wasn't the one in danger of being targeted by the ghouls.

Drew cleared his throat. "I'll get a team together and bring them back to the inn."

"Preferably without telling Petra," I muttered. "Though I hope Maurice is quick to tell the police what he knows about the tunnel."

"He will be," Tam said over his shoulder as he made for the door. "Coming, Perry?"

"All right." She gave me a guilty look and then followed her team.

The door slid closed behind them. I watched, half hoping one of them would come back, until a flash of light drew my eyes away. Allie had her wand out, casting a spell on the bar to clear up the remaining mud.

"You didn't have to do that," I protested. "I'm the one who made a mess of the place."

"You didn't," Carey said. "The ghoul did—and it's not alone, is it? I heard what you said. There's a nest by the river."

"I'm their target." That much was clear. "You and Allie should go and wait somewhere safe. Get into a room and put sage in front of the door. That'll keep them out. In fact, we should do the same to the guests' rooms too."

I wished Jia hadn't already left, but dragging her back here now would only make her into a potential target too.

"All right." Allie beckoned to Carey. "We'll go upstairs and get the sage. I kept some for emergencies, but the ghosts… I don't want to scare them off either."

"I'll warn the ghosts, and I'll ask them to keep an eye on the river to help out," I decided. "You two go upstairs—and let me know if you hear or see anything else."

The only ghost currently in the room was Mart, who made a rude noise. "I'm not playing security guard."

"I never said you had to." I walked through the lobby to the games room in search of the other ghosts, but the room was empty.

"They're probably hiding." Mart drifted in behind me. "I doubt they'll come out if you're going to throw sage everywhere."

"How else am I supposed to stop the ghouls from getting inside?" His attitude problem did nothing to help my apprehension. "This is serious. There're at least three more ghouls lurking under the bridge."

"And you couldn't even deal with one."

"You don't have to rub it in." My bruised knees were proof enough, and I hoped my pain spell would hold out long enough for me to get rid of the ghouls' nest. "I'll figure something out when Drew's team gets here. Ghouls are scared of Reapers, so I have that going for me, but I need to stop them from getting at the others."

For that reason, I knew they hadn't come here of their own volition. In fact, there was a fair chance the person who'd brought them here was lurking under the bridge herself, waiting for me to come and hunt her down.

"That Mina Devlin is really persistent." Mart voiced the name I hadn't yet spoken aloud. "You're in trouble this time."

"Again, I don't need to hear that."

"I wasn't making fun." He sounded earnest, for a wonder. "Are you sure you want to send Drew and his team up against her?"

No. "Until Petra stops holding the Wardens hostage on bogus charges, we don't have a choice."

"You don't think *she* brought the ghouls here?"

"Of course she didn't." Yet a sliver of doubt had lodged in my mind. "Petra's a witch, not a necromancer, and she can't see ghosts, either."

"I notice you didn't start with 'a police officer wouldn't break the law.'"

"Yeah, but she wants me out of town, not dead." I dragged my gaze away from the empty games room. "Right. I'll find the ghosts…"

"No, I will."

"You aren't going to demand I get down on my knees and beg for your help?"

Mart grinned. "If you want to, feel free. It'll be funny."

"Honestly." I rolled my eyes at him. "I'm sorry if I made you feel like I was ignoring you. For the record, I don't completely trust the Wardens, either, but they're our best shot at stopping the ghouls from overrunning the place."

"I'll find the other ghosts." He floated out of the games room ahead of me. "The other ghouls won't get anywhere near the inn."

Not if I have anything to do with it, I thought, heading for the stairs. I kept my stash of sage and other herbs in a box under my bed so it wouldn't irritate Mart or the other ghosts, though I was occasionally tempted to use it to keep him from disturbing Drew and me. Glad I'd stocked up recently, I grabbed several bags of herbs and stuffed them into my pocket.

As I ran out of my room, I nearly collided with Carey outside the door. "Maura—what's that?"

"Sage," I replied. "I'm going to bolster our defences. Did your mum tell you to go to your room?"

"Yes, but I don't want to hide." Her hands clenched. "Not when you're risking your life out there."

"I'm the Reaper. It goes with the territory," I said. "Besides, I won't be alone. Drew and his team will be here soon… and hopefully the Wardens too. Until they arrive, the ghosts will help me protect the inn."

She didn't look entirely convinced. "But you're not going to hunt the ghouls alone, are you?"

"No, I'm not," I said. "Drew's bringing a team, and we'll drive off the ghouls. Can you and your mum hide out until then?"

She nodded slowly. "All right."

Hoping she would stay in her room, I made my way downstairs to the lobby. Although I knew Drew would do his best to recruit people to help, I was equally confident Petra would stand in his way at every turn. She'd already held up the Wardens indefinitely, and while she might not be on the side of the ghouls, she wouldn't lift a finger to stop them from attacking me.

That left me with one choice... I had to defend the inn myself.

14

I walked downstairs to find the other ghosts milling around the lobby. My brother had kept his word, although all the spirits except Mart recoiled when they saw the bags of sage in my hands.

"I'm not putting it inside the inn," I told them. "This is to put outside in case the ghouls get too close. We don't want any more of those monsters getting inside, do we?"

"Definitely not," Mart said. "Come on, you can handle a bit of sage, can't you?"

I hoped so, because the ghosts would be my only allies against the ghouls until the backup got here, which might take hours for all I knew. Leaving my brother to convince the other ghosts they wouldn't be harmed, I carried the sage outside into the drizzly cold, where the sky had darkened fully in the past hour or so. The ghouls would be out to feed soon… including their newest recruit.

I had to admit, I hoped the ghoul in the morgue transformed sooner rather than later. That way, the Wardens would have unequivocal proof of Maurice's innocence and would be free to help me destroy its nest without Petra and the others getting in the way—assuming the ghoul didn't escape under the police's noses because Petra was too busy distracting them with nonsense, of course. She might not be on Mina Devlin's side, but she was a thorn in my side, and I had little doubt we'd have a reckoning of our own sooner or later.

Mart drifted up to me as I began laying the sage around the front door. "That's not going to stop the ghouls from coming in through the back entrance. Or the windows."

"I'm aware of that." The front doors faced the river, and if the ghouls were coming from the bridge, they'd be more likely to come in through this route. "I'll put the rest around the bridge."

My phone began buzzing as I finished laying sage in front of the doors, and I fished it out of my pocket. "Hey, Drew. Did you get the team together?"

"I hit a snag," he said. "We got a call from the Wardens' head office. Seems they wanted to check up on their team."

"You're joking, aren't you?"

"Unfortunately not."

"Mina Devlin." *Or one of her allies, which is pretty much the same.* "She manufactured a distraction."

"It might not be. The Wardens are sticklers for the rules."

"What are the odds of this happening at this very instant, though?" I ground my teeth. "Please tell me Maurice at least had the chance to tell the rest of the police that the ghouls are hiding under the bridge."

"He's still with Petra in the questioning room."

"Seriously?" She was dragging this out, and she wouldn't care if the inn was overrun by ghouls in the interim. "Has the other ghoul transformed yet?"

"Not that I'm aware of," he said, "but the other Wardens were keeping watch before we got the call."

"Of course they were." I swore. "The ghouls aren't going

to stop with the inn, you know. Let Petra know that too. I wonder if *her* call history shows anything interesting?"

"Huh?" His voice quieted to almost a whisper. "You think she called the Wardens? Really?"

"It wouldn't surprise me." Cold water slid down my hand as the sky upended itself on my head, dousing my last shreds of patience. "In fact, I'm almost certain she's the one who put in the initial report, in the hopes that they'd send another team who'd report me to their superiors and get me arrested."

"What?" Disbelief bled into his tone. "That's not possible, Maura. She couldn't have known the recent disappearances had any connection to a monster that would require the Wardens' involvement."

"Either that, or Mina Devlin called them like last time," I said, "but I have my doubts. She failed once already, and this team actually has their priorities straight."

Or they had before the police ensured they were distracted by pointless bureaucracy. I adjusted my grip on my damp phone, listening to Drew's silence as he considered my words. "Maura… you aren't outside, are you?"

"I'm setting up sage around the inn."

"Maura."

"I don't see any ghouls." I lifted my head and spied someone approaching across the bridge. *Ack. Famous last words.* "Can you hang on a moment?"

"Maura, what's going on?" His voice faded out as I moved the phone away from my ear and peered at the bridge to see who was approaching. Not a ghoul but a person. Perry.

"Does Tam know you ran off?" I called to her.

"I convinced him to let me come back," Perry replied. "I pointed out that Maurice doesn't like me enough to care whether I'm there to give him moral support and that it makes no sense for our entire team to wait for a single ghoul while there's a whole nest of them waiting to attack elsewhere."

"Maura?" Drew's voice grew louder when I lifted the phone to my ear again. "Is that Perry?"

"Yeah, she must have come back to help." I drew in a breath. "Can you remind Petra and the other officers of their priorities—and the Wardens' head office, too, if you have the chance to speak to them?"

"I will, but the Wardens' supervisors outrank me. Perry must have left the police station before they called."

"You won't tell the others where she is, will you?" I didn't need to ask, and he didn't need to answer. He was the only member of the police force I currently trusted. "Talk later?"

"All right." Reluctance underlaid his voice, but he knew that if he didn't get a team together fast, Perry and I were more likely to end up fighting the ghouls alone. "See you soon, Maura."

Perry eyed the bag of sage in my hand as I ended the call. "Isn't that going to scare off the ghosts?"

"Not if I put it out here." I pocketed my phone and showed her what was left of the sage. "It'd be easier if I knew where the tunnel's entrance was so I could stop the ghouls from getting out, but I might as well make their lives difficult in any way I can."

"Maurice said the nest was directly underneath the bridge," she replied. "That's what I came to check out, but why would the ghouls make their nest right next to running water? Seems unlikely."

"Unlikely but not impossible." Yes, I'd told Carey and Drew that I had no intention of going in there alone, but *looking* for the nest didn't count. "It'll ruin their night if I stop them getting out of their nest altogether."

"I'd sooner set the nest on fire, but I don't have a spell for that."

"What was that disintegration spell you and Farley used earlier?"

"It only works on dead things," she said. "We'd have to get inside the nest to use it on the ghouls, and there's no guarantee we'd get out again."

"There is that." I resumed sprinkling sage across the ground. "Whereabouts did Maurice say the tunnel's other entrance is? It comes out somewhere, doesn't it?"

"I'm not sure where it comes out, but the entrance we're looking for is right down there." She indicated the sloping riverbank. "Must be well hidden."

"Must be, considering nobody knew it was there," I said. "Including Allie and Carey, who've lived here forever."

"They've never had reason to go poking around under the bridge, have they?"

"Well, no, but how did even the police have no idea it was there?" It wasn't as if this was the first time there'd been trouble near the river... though not at this end of town, admittedly, and the inn had been all but forgotten by the other residents of Hawkwood Hollow before I'd moved here.

"Werewolves don't like being underground," Perry suggested. "Might that be why?"

"Not all the police are werewolves." No, the only explanation was that the tunnel hadn't been in use until recently... which increased the already-towering odds of a certain person's involvement.

After we'd covered the area with sage, Perry and I approached the riverbank. There was no path underneath the bridge leading to the tunnel's entrance, but when Perry reached the water's edge, she poked one booted foot into the water.

"What—what are you doing?" *Does she not know how strong those currents are?*

"Maurice said it's not too deep along here." She pulled out

her wand and pointed it at the water. "I'll slow the currents down, but it doesn't look that bad tonight."

"Would Maurice find it funny if you ended up stranded under the bridge after the spell wears off?" Over my dead body was *I* getting into the water, but Perry had both feet in now and seemed intent on wading right through the currents.

"Well, yes, but if he can get through here, so can I." She gave a sudden yelp as the water surged up to her knees. "Okay, there's a drop here."

"If you drown, I'm not being responsible for breaking the news to your team. They'd blame me."

"Nah, they'll know it was my idea, but you don't have to worry about that." She waded underneath the bridge's shadow, lifting her wand and conjuring a light. "Hey... there's our ghoul nest."

"You already found it?" Despite my instincts telling me to turn back, I slid down the muddy bank into the water, grimacing when the coldness washed over my feet and up to my ankles.

Ahead of me, Perry's wand illuminated the area under the tunnel... and a distinct gap in the packed earth of the river-bank. A tunnel-entrance-sized gap.

"How'd the ghouls get out of there without going into the water?" I waded after her, hissing out a breath when I hit the spot where the ground sloped and the water lapped up to my knees.

"I don't know... wait." Perry stiffened. "Do you feel like we're being watched?"

"I do now." I moved to her side, joining her underneath the bridge. The hairs on the back of my neck stood on end, and my skin prickled at a faint dripping sound. *Yeah... now I feel it.*

Lifting my head, I saw movement stirring in the shadowy

underside of the bridge above our heads. Perry's light flickered up, and my breath caught. Several dark shapes clung to the underside of the bridge. *Ghouls. Of course... they can climb.*

I held my breath, reaching for my wand. I'd have grabbed the sage, too, but the ghouls were too far out of reach to hit from this angle without a wand.

Perry remained silent, her gaze fixed on the ceiling, as if she were thinking as hard as I was. The instant either of us moved, the ghouls might jump at us—or worse, scrabble up to the surface and attack the inn. I'd only put sage around the front doors and the front of the bridge, not realising those creepy monsters could simply climb up the sides.

I backed up a step, water swirling around my legs, and the distinct sound of footsteps sounded on the bridge above our heads.

Perry sucked in a breath. "Someone's up there."

"Let's hope they're on our side," I murmured.

Or not, because they had no idea of the threat beneath their feet unless we shouted and gave ourselves away. The ghouls stirred at the sound of footsteps, and then one of them began to crawl along the underside of the bridge like an incredibly ugly version of Spiderman.

"Oh no, you don't." I held up my hands, calling the shadows of the afterworld to my fingertips, but the ghouls were too far off to be threatened by my magic.

As the ghoul disappeared up the side of the bridge, someone screamed. As if released from a spell, the other ghouls moved, following its lead. One, though, jumped straight for Perry and me, claws outstretched.

Perry lifted her wand, and her spell struck the ghoul in midair. The beast plunged into the water, and I raised a hand to shield my face from the splash. "That wasn't smart."

"Ghouls aren't smart," she returned. "I can knock some of the others off too."

"Might be too late." The others were already scrambling up onto the bridge to attack the newcomers. Turning my back on the tunnel entrance, I waded out from under the bridge. Dealing with the nest would have to wait until later.

As Perry joined me, someone called down to us from above. "Are you down there? Perry?"

"Tam!" she exclaimed. "Watch out for the ghouls!"

Tam's back? Did the police let Maurice go? I didn't dare hope we'd get that lucky, but I waded out of the water as quickly as humanly possible and ran up the bank. Or tried to. My wet feet slid in the mud, my panic rising as the sound of the other Wardens fighting the oncoming ghouls echoed from the bridge.

"Need a hand?" Perry emerged from the water beside me and leapt up the bank with far more athleticism than I possessed.

"No." I called the shadows instead and leapt into the after-world, picturing the bridge in my mind's eye.

I landed in the midst of utter chaos. Callum was back in his werewolf form, grappling with one of the ghouls, while Farley and Tam fought another. Most surprisingly of all, the vampire stood on the other side of the bridge.

"The police let you go?" I called to him.

Maurice ignored me and lunged at one of the ghouls clambering up the bridge. Unable to cross the water himself, he was still more than a match for the ghoul's speed. The two grappled with one another with such ferocity that it was hard to see who had the upper hand until Maurice rose upright, the ghoul lying dead at his feet.

Two ghouls down, at least three to go. As another climbed along the bridge, I called the shadows and punched it with a shadowy fist. It fell off the edge then disappeared into the surging waters.

Where did they all come from? There were more than five,

more than the number of bodies that should have been in their nest. This had been going on for longer than we knew… and the only way to find out the true extent of the ghouls' forces was to go back under the bridge and face whatever awaited us inside their nest.

15

The ghoul I'd punched vanished beneath the dark waters, while I saw Perry and Farley casting spells at another beast that had clawed its way out from the river.

"I thought they didn't like water." I hurried over to join them as the ghoul began to slither up the bank, dodging their spells.

"I guess it doesn't count as crossing the water if they fall into it." Perry fired another spell, which missed when the ghoul cleared the bank in a lunge, only to recoil away from the pile of sage I'd dropped at the bridge's edge. *Ha.*

I gave chase, my phone buzzing in my pocket. Drew, I was willing to bet. Hoping that meant he'd managed to ditch Petra and was ready to bring reinforcements, I summoned shadows to my palm to fend off the ghoul. "Get out of here!"

As I took aim, light flashed from Perry's wand, and the ghoul vanished in an explosion of dust.

"Thanks," I said over my shoulder, fishing my phone from my pocket. "Damn creatures are fast."

"You don't mind me destroying this one?" she asked. "Joking, joking."

I checked my phone. Two missed calls from Drew. "Did the ghoul at the morgue transform? Do you know?"

"Not sure. Tam's a bit tied up at the moment."

I glanced up at the bridge, where Tam was single-handedly grappling with a ghoul, some kind of weapon in his hand. He clearly had the upper hand from his position, but I counted at least five new monsters clambering up the edges.

Where'd they come from? Someone had been working on this for a while—that was for sure. With one hand, I called Drew back, keeping an eye on the ongoing struggle with the ghouls in case one of them tried to sneak up on me from behind.

The phone rang, once, twice, three times. Now *he* wasn't replying. My gaze went to Perry, who'd slid down the riverbank again.

"What are you doing?" I asked her.

"Getting rid of their nest." She held up her wand. "I have a spell that can blast through solid rock."

"Hang on—you don't want to blow up the bridge too." That wouldn't do anyone any favours, including her own team.

"I won't." She waded into the shallows for the second time. Grimacing, I reluctantly followed her slippery path down the riverbank again.

"Perry," I hissed. "I'm serious. This river is... It's volatile. It's flooded before."

"I'm not going to flood the river, Maura," she told me. "Don't you want to get rid of the ghouls?"

"Of course I do, but I'm pretty sure the person who brought them here in the first place would *love* a flood to distract everyone's attention so she can use it as a diversion to come back and make everyone's lives a misery."

"Who?" She slowed her pace, water lapping around her ankles. "This witch who has it in for you?"

"She's a former coven leader," I replied. "She's spent the past few months trying to manufacture ways to either get me arrested or kicked out of town, or else to distract everyone's attention so she can get back to her so-called rightful position."

"Someone needs to get a life."

"Well, she is a fugitive thanks to me." I lifted my head to peer up at the bridge. "Did Tam give you permission to come down here alone?"

"None of the others want to go into the water." She began wading again, lifting her wand to slow the currents. "Why are you so certain it'll flood?"

"Because," I murmured, "the last floods weren't an accident. It's been over twenty years, and most of the town doesn't know the truth, but it's why the Reaper retired. His apprentice was one of the people who got killed in the aftermath."

She stopped walking. "Wait. Is *that* why the town's full of ghosts?"

"Yes, it is." I might have questioned the wisdom of telling an outsider the depth of Mina Devlin's depravity, but she'd gone too far this time. Moreover, the tunnels were far more than a nest for ghouls. I was willing to bet my nonexistent scythe on it. "We don't have any proof, but a tunnel that's been hidden under the river since the floods might give us a shot at finding some hard evidence."

Or it might lead us to Mina Devlin herself. Would Perry's teammates have second thoughts about her venturing into the ghouls' nest if they knew who else we might find in there? I had to remind myself that Perry had volunteered for this mission herself; her teammates didn't dictate her choices.

If they didn't want to go underground—and hell, *I* didn't either—we'd have to hope the two of us would bring enough firepower to get rid of the ghouls' nest *and* its creator.

"That's why you don't want it to be destroyed?" Perry inclined her head. "I get it."

"Seems like we shouldn't risk exploding anything with your teammates standing above our heads anyway." I followed her lead, shuddering when the cold water washed up my ankles and then higher. "I should have worn a wetsuit."

"It's only a little water." She waded ahead of me and then lifted her wand's light to point at the underside of the bridge. "There aren't any more ghouls up there. Hope that means there's none in their nest either."

"What are the odds of that?"

"Less reliable than I'd like." She waited for me to catch up, shining her wand's light over the earthen wall beneath the bridge. The tunnel's entrance was narrow enough that if the river's waters had been any higher, it would be impossible to spot. Not to mention flooded.

Is that how it was hidden? Underwater? I hadn't noticed the river's waters were any lower than usual, especially when it had been raining so much recently, but it was certainly possible for a witch of Mina Devlin's capacity to subtly mess with the river's currents without anyone noticing. She wouldn't have needed to be inside the town herself to do it either.

"It's barely big enough for one of us to get into." I indicated the hole in the ground. "And what're the chances of us being able to climb out again? We don't have claws."

From this angle, I couldn't even see the bottom. At the thought of being trapped underground while ghouls ran overhead and Mina Devlin hunted us down, a shiver ran down my spine that had nothing to do with the icy water lapping against my legs.

Perry tilted her head. "Can't you use your Reaper powers to get pretty much anywhere?"

"Yes, but I don't typically take passengers along." Perry herself didn't have any unique powers that I knew of. She was fast and clearly knowledgeable on both magic and the monsters of the afterworld, but that wouldn't save her from getting stuck in a tunnel and starving to death.

"But you *can* carry another person?"

"If said other person doesn't blow up the walls and cause the tunnel to cave in, yes."

She shot me a wry smile. "Noted. I'm going in."

Perry scrambled onto the narrow stretch of earth underneath the sloping wall, standing on tiptoe to peer in.

"Can you see the bottom?" I asked her.

"Yeah… should be able to get in without any trouble." Perry drew back and made a jump for the tunnel entrance. Her feet skidded in the mud instead of disappearing into the tunnel. Her arms wheeled, and she caught her balance before she fell into the water. On her second attempt, she made it in, vanishing into the hollow darkness.

"Erm… Perry?" I called to her. "Are you okay?"

"Sure—there's a solid landing." Her head poked out of the hole. "Coming?"

"Right." No sense in wasting time. I attempted to climb up to the entrance like Perry had, but my freezing feet were too clumsy to keep my balance, and I slid straight back down again. The coldness of the afterworld had nothing on the river, and even the heat of embarrassment didn't stop the risk of hypothermia.

After my second failed attempt to climb into the nest, Perry extended a hand. I fought back my prevailing instincts and reached out to let her pull me into the tunnel. My feet touched down on solid ground, and her wand illuminated the narrow passage ahead.

"I'll lead the way," I offered. "If there's a trap up ahead, it's less likely to work on me than it is on you."

"Well… All right." With obvious reluctance, she stepped back to let me overtake her. "Hmm… Do you think it's a good idea to use a spell to widen the tunnel?"

"Please don't." The passage might be narrow, but the roof and walls appeared reassuringly solid. This wasn't a hand-dug tunnel but a carefully built passage—whether by magic or by manual labour, I didn't know.

"Only joking." She began to follow my lead since there wasn't enough room for us to walk side by side. I had to duck my head under the low ceiling, while the sound of my chattering teeth echoed off the walls.

"Want me to use a drying spell?" she asked.

I shook my head. "No point. We have to go back through the river to get out."

Unless I did use my Reaper powers as a shortcut, but even someone as unflappable as Perry might be cowed by a trip through the afterworld. I'd keep that in reserve in case we did get stuck in here, but it would strictly be a last resort.

After a short distance, the tunnel widened. The walls became stone rather than earth. Rocks lay scattered on the floor, and a sharp tang in the air stung my nostrils.

Perry sniffed too. "Someone used a spell in here."

"Yeah." I watched the light of her wand illuminate markings on the walls, the signs of complex magic. "Might be a booby trap."

"I don't think it is." She moved closer to the nearest wall, her gaze roving over the damp stone. "The spell is defunct. It's old."

"Smells recent." I sniffed again, scanning the wall for more symbols. While the ones we'd initially found were worn with age, others were newer. Faint light trickled through the marks etched into the stone. Yet whether old or new, the symbols were all the same—a line of five glyphs, repeated over and over.

"This is a sealing spell," Perry murmured. "I've seen it before… but who's been reapplying it?"

"Reapplying?"

"There's no way to make that spell permanent," she said in explanation. "If someone sealed this place off, they'll have known the spell wouldn't last."

"So they kept reapplying it." *Mina Devlin.* I couldn't picture her traipsing around hidden tunnels while she was the coven leader, but she could easily have volunteered one of her fellow coven members for the honour if most of her supporters hadn't been in jail. That must be why the passage had reopened, potentially for the first time in over twenty years.

No wonder it had never been discovered beforehand if Mina's supporters had been ensuring the passage remained hidden. Yet why would she have let the ghouls move in here? If this place contained some evidence that she hadn't wanted us to find, leaving the tunnel open didn't make any sense. Unless she'd assumed I wouldn't come looking for their nest, but I would have thought Mina would have wanted to cover all her bases.

I spied another narrow tunnel opening nearby, with another large chamber beyond. Perry sucked in a breath, gesturing at something that lay on the ground ahead. Bones. There were bodies still down here. My skin crawled. Were they victims of the flood or more recent? There was no way to tell, so I forced myself to continue through to the second chamber. *Where's that ghoul nest? Or did they all leave to attack us?*

A faint but unmistakable clattering noise came from

behind us. Perry halted, twisting around with her wand light in hand. "There's someone in here."

"Who?" I spun around, too, as a dazzling light erupted in the chamber we'd left behind. The light burned my eyes, forcing me to squeeze them shut. "Hey! Show yourself!"

Nobody answered, but Perry's muffled curse prompted me to open my eyes a fraction. She'd tried to back out of the tunnel, only to halt in her tracks as if she'd crashed into a brick wall. "The spell was still active."

"What?" I shuffled backwards, my feet fetching up against an invisible barrier. When I squinted at it, I could see a shimmering light overlaying the way out of the tunnel and into the chamber we'd left behind.

"Should have seen that one coming." Perry craned her neck, but there was no sign of who'd reactivated the spell. "We'll have to keep going. There's got to be another passage somewhere ahead."

"What're the odds that one's blocked too?" I didn't wait for an answer; Perry and I both knew we didn't have much choice but to move on, continuing through the narrow tunnel towards whatever trap Mina had left for us next.

When we entered the next chamber, the light of Perry's wand went out. "What the—"

A flickering green light ahead of us drew my eyes to the walls, upon which more marks were etched. "Another spell? Can you tell what it is?"

"It's… It's some kind of countermagic charm." Perry stumbled forward, no longer as sure-footed without any light to see by. "I think it killed my light charm. I bet they only want us to use their source of illumination."

"Figures." I was comfortable in darkness, but I hated knowing I was walking into a trap without the use of all of my senses. And while I could use the afterworld to get out, part of me recoiled at the notion of fleeing like a coward. "If you're here, Mina Devlin, come out and face me."

A scuffling answered, then Perry shrieked, falling to the ground. I hit out blindly, my fist connecting with a slippery surface that could only be a ghoul's face. "Ow!"

"Get off me!" Perry's wand blasted the ghoul back, but her spell had the unintended effect of the beast landing on top of me instead.

My knees folded as the monster's wriggling body landed on me, and a painful throb rang through my legs. *Ow. The spell must have killed my pain-relief charm too.*

Losing patience, I called the shadows, and my fist connected with the monster's skull so hard that pain vibrated up my arm. "Ow."

That shouldn't have hurt. What the hell is going on? The pain in my legs made it hard to think clearly, but Perry's next spell struck the ghoul in the back. The monster's body briefly lit up in fiery light before it crumbled to ashes.

I brushed the ashes off me, my hand throbbing. "Here's a tip. Don't punch a ghoul in the face."

"Didn't you use your magic?"

"I thought I did." I reached for my Reaper powers again, but the darkness inside the room was solid enough that I couldn't tell it apart from the afterworld.

Perry cleared her throat. "Ah, does that suppressant spell work on your powers too?"

"It shouldn't…" But there was another possibility. "The coven *has* been working on a spell that counters my Reaper abilities. Last time, they used a booby trap that hit me when I touched it by accident."

"You're joking, aren't you? Is that even possible?"

"These people don't play by the rules." I reached for my wand, for all the good that did, trying to suppress the panic rising in my chest. If my Reaper powers weren't working *and* the way ahead was blocked, we couldn't get out. Not even through the afterworld.

"Maura?" Perry's usually steady voice wavered a little. "C'mon. The only way out is through, right?"

"Right?" I did my best to squash down the tide of fear inside me. "Perry, can you cast a spell-removal charm on me? That's what worked last time."

"Sure, if you keep still." A brief light flashed from her wand, but between my throbbing fist and aching legs, I felt nothing but pain. Heart in my throat, I reached for the shadows and grasped nothing but air.

Mina must have fine-tuned her booby-trap spell. "Try a different counterspell."

"Okay." Another flash of light followed, and once again, I tried to use my Reaper powers—with no effect. "I only know three spells… unless we tried a more complex one, but it's tricky enough to use in daylight."

I wasn't expert enough to know all the varieties of removal spell, but there was a limit on what one could achieve with only a wand. Let alone in a dark underground chamber with a suppressant spell etched into the walls. I heard Perry fumbling in her pocket behind me. "You aren't going to blow up the wall, are you?"

"Nah, those spells won't work on a wall that's reinforced with defensive magic. I'm going to text Tam."

"Will your phone even work down here?"

"It might." Even her phone's screen seemed dimmer than usual when she turned it on, and the only other light came from the flickering symbols on the walls. A dripping sounded in the background as she sent her message, and when Perry put away her phone, I reached out with a hand to feel my way forward along the wall.

"There's got to be a way out of this chamber." I shuffled onward, my feet skidding on the damp floor. I didn't like the idea of holding onto the spell-covered walls for balance, but it was that or trip over my own feet—or the bones of the last people to set foot into this chamber.

Not a helpful thought. Teeth gritted, I felt my way around the edge of the chamber, the dripping noise growing even more noticeable in the wider space.

"Hey! There's another tunnel over there." Perry nudged me from behind, turning me in the right direction. "It's the only way ahead, I think."

The dripping continued as we hesitantly made our way onward, not at all helped by our total inability to see where we were going. A crushing sense of despair hung over me like a raincloud. As if my thoughts had conjured up an actual raincloud, the dripping intensified, drowning out Perry's next words. Literally. Icy dampness washed over my feet as my shoes sloshed in sudden ankle-deep water. "Is that coming from ahead of us?"

"No, it's in here." Perry grabbed my arm and pulled me after her. "We have to get out."

We ducked into the tunnel, feeling our way forward by gripping the walls on either side, as the sound of rushing water filled the chamber behind us. *Oh, dammit.*

"You've got to be kidding me," I gasped.

Water hit the backs of my legs, and we ran. Or rather, waded. The tunnel had only one way forward, but with every step, the water climbed higher. I snarled under my breath as the current reached my waist, forcing me to tread water to keep from being swept away.

I would *not* die down here in the darkness, helpless and hunted.

Kicking my feet, I swam, propelled by the surging current, my hands occasionally knocking into Perry's shoulders as we carried onward. *This tunnel must come to an end somewhere.*

Then Perry came to a sudden halt. "No… not again."

"What?"

She treaded water, cursing under her breath. "There's something blocking the way."

"What?" I attempted to swim past her, but my hand touched a solid barrier too. I couldn't see the spell creating the barrier in front of us, but there was no doubt it was there.

"We're stuck." Panic rose in Perry's voice. "I'm sorry. I should have told you… I'm cursed."

"You're cursed?" I echoed. "What is this? A last-minute deathbed confession?"

"Yeah, I'm cursed with eternal bad luck," she said. "A curse which tends to get people who come into contact with me killed."

"That would have been useful to know earlier." Icy water lapped at my neck, while my feet were utterly numb. "Wait. What about your teammates? Wouldn't that make them into targets too?"

"They've been lucky to escape so far, as long as they haven't tried to follow us." She drew in a shaky breath. "Got any confessions?"

"You've already heard mine." I'd told her more about the cause of the flood and my clash with Mina Devlin than most people knew, but the rest wasn't my secret to tell. "Except…"

"What?" Her breath came out in pants. "I'm not going to be able to tell anyone now, am I?"

"Except…" I swallowed. "I brought my brother back from the afterworld and bound him to me when he died."

"You did?" Awe filled her voice. "Wait. doesn't that mean he'll die if you do? Permanently, I mean?"

"Yes. It does." *Poor Mart.* He had no idea I was here nor that my death approached with every passing moment.

Wait. I might be without my Reaper powers, but my brother and I remained bound together. Could I reach him, even in here? I closed my eyes, conscious of the water creeping up to my chin. The afterworld was beyond my reach, but Mart was bound to *me*, not to the afterworld itself.

Mart! I thought, then spoke aloud. "Mart!"

My voice echoed off the walls, and then water rushed over my head, leaving the sound of my own scream echoing in my ears. Darkness, absolute darkness, filled my entire world, smothering my other senses.

Was this what Mart had seen before I brought him back from death? *Mart, please, hear me. I can't get out of here without you.*

Maura?

The voice rang in my head and through the tunnel, startling me. *Mart? Are you there?*

Yes—where are you?

In the tunnel under the bridge, but the tunnels in and out are both blocked by a spell. I can't get out, and you can't get in.

You should have more faith in me.

Huh?

There's nowhere I can't get into. His laughter filled my head, and then someone grabbed my wrist. I kicked out, hearing Perry's muffled voice. "Whoa, there. I'm trying to help."

She seized my wrist again, and my head broke the surface of the water. I coughed uncontrollably, complete blackness encasing me on all sides even though I could feel Perry's arm next to mine. "What—"

"There's a little breathing room up here," Perry murmured from nearby. "Not much, but enough."

"My brother—" I coughed. "He heard me, but he can't get in."

"Can't he? Isn't he a ghost?"

Wait. The spell was designed to keep people out, but most spells didn't apply to the dead. He might be able to get in after all, but he couldn't get us *out*. His own Reaper abilities were limited, and if someone living helped him, they'd meet the same end as the pair of us.

I sucked in another shallow breath, my forehead brushing the tunnel's ceiling. Another inch or two of water would finish off both of us, and while Reapers couldn't drown, half-Reapers weren't as resilient. Especially ones without access to their powers.

She planned for this. Mina did. I counted my breaths, focusing on the mental image of Mina's smirking face to keep from giving up, from letting my numb legs win and the water draw me into its embrace again.

My stupor broke when a sudden glow lit up the air. In front of me, Perry startled. Eyes as round as saucers, she reached out a hand, straight through the invisible barrier.

Did someone turn off the barrier spells? My heart lifted despite myself, but we'd found the only breathing spot in the tunnel. To get out, we'd have to dive below the water again.

"How far is it to the exit, do you think?" I whispered to Perry. "Can we swim?"

"I don't think we have much choice." Water lapped up to her chin as she drew in a long breath. "Ready?"

No. I still couldn't sense my Reaper abilities, but they might take a bit longer to come back on than the use of regular magic. In any case, I wasn't taking any chances.

I sucked in air then dove below the water once more. The faint glow from the walls was bright enough to light the way ahead but not much else, and the seconds stretched out as Perry and I swam through the tunnel. *There has to be an end somewhere.* But Maurice hadn't said *where* the other entrance was, and it might be next to the river itself for all I knew. That would make sense, given how quickly the chamber had flooded, but it would be a bitter irony to escape the tunnel only to drown in the river's unforgiving currents.

My lungs burned with each moment. Perry kicked ahead

of me. The narrow passage darkened as we left the wards behind—and still, no end appeared in sight. My legs screamed, my vision blurring as my oxygen ran out. Then Perry jerked to a halt, and I crashed into her. Through the blurry haze, I glimpsed what appeared to be a person in the water, grabbing Perry's arm and pulling her after. *Fast.*

I didn't have a voice to ask questions with or any breath to spare, but my only companion had vanished. A light shone ahead, smothered by the black dots dancing across my vision as the last of my strength began to fade.

Mart's face appeared before my eyes, so starkly clear that he might have been right next to me, and he stared at me through the wavering darkness. "Don't you dare. Don't you even think about dragging me down with you."

I seized the last ounce of strength I possessed and kicked again and again. My head broke the surface in a rush, and I gasped, cold air flooding in. My blurred vision showed two figures at the edge of the river—it *was* the river. I pushed myself in that direction until the water came to an end, and I collapsed onto the muddy shore.

Lifting my head to survey my rescuers, I gasped out, "I didn't know vampires could swim."

Maurice, sitting on the riverbank with a shivering Perry at his feet, simply gave me a sarcastic look in response. A laugh drew my eyes to my brother, who floated beside them.

"It really is you," I croaked. "You... You came back."

"Obviously," he said. "Did you think I'd let you drown? Who else would listen to the sound of my divine singing voice?"

Luckily, I passed out before he began singing the Pokémon theme tune again.

"I told you," I said impatiently, "the ghouls didn't come here of their own accord. They didn't pick their nest location by accident either."

"A tunnel." Petra made a sceptical noise from the other side of the desk in the room at the police station. "You expect us to believe that a tunnel mysteriously showed up under the river that's never been noticed beforehand?"

"Nobody noticed it because it was covered up." I shivered, having woken up with a full-blown cold that morning after my unexpected diving lesson the previous night. In the chair next to me, Perry kept sneezing too. "When the river's water levels are a bit lower, you can have a look and see for yourself."

"Also, someone used a spell to seal us in there," Perry said hoarsely. "There were already sealing spells all over the walls —lots of them. Someone's been resealing the tunnels over and over, for years."

"Really." Her tone was flat. "Why would someone do that?"

"I don't know, but I have a suspect." I coughed. "Someone

who the police ought to be looking for instead of interrogating us."

"That's enough." Her nostrils flared. "Ghouls like the cold and damp, you said. That means it's only natural that they'd live near the river."

"They weren't near the river. They were underground."

At least she'd been forced to accept the ghouls' existence after the body at the morgue had tried to strangle the unfortunate supervisor watching over it. Drew had told me that the ghoul's attempted escape had been shortly before my excursion into the tunnels, but I was still cobbling together what had happened elsewhere in town while I'd been down there. I'd already been unconscious when the police had shown up.

"Why don't you believe us?" asked Perry. "There's a lot of abandoned buildings near the river. Surely a hidden series of tunnels isn't that much of a stretch."

"Exactly," I said. "The whole area was abandoned during the floods."

"You weren't even here," Petra said dismissively. "You'd have been a child then."

I bristled. "I'm aware of that, but I don't need to have been here to make the obvious connection. There were bodies down there. Humans."

"The bodies of the victims?"

"No… I don't think so." I shuddered at the thought. "They were skeletons. They'd been there for years."

"That's not relevant to your report, is it?"

"I thought you wanted to know about the tunnels," I said. "Also, it's Tam who has to give a report to the Wardens, not me."

"If we were lying, we wouldn't have mentioned the tunnels in our official report," Perry added. "The Wardens' head office scrutinises every detail."

"Do they now?" A hint of calculation entered her tone, and a suspicion reared its head inside me before sinking into weary resignation. Even if I turned out to be right about her role in contacting the Wardens, I had no energy left for another confrontation. Besides, if the Wardens *did* come to examine the tunnels, it would be a hindrance to Mina's plans, which could only be a good thing.

We'd have to wait for the water levels to subside before venturing inside again, but I had a pile of questions that the tunnels alone could answer. How Mina Devlin had cut off my Reaper powers, for instance. Had someone cast the spell on me, or had it been among the ones etched into the tunnel walls? The latter was more likely, but it was clear that Mina or one of her allies had been in the tunnels shortly before Perry and I were. That didn't necessarily mean they'd been in Hawkwood Hollow itself, though. The tunnel's other entrance, as it turned out, was far enough down the river that it was surrounded by fields. It would have been nice if Maurice had mentioned that sooner, but according to Perry, he hadn't expected us to get stuck in there.

I hadn't even had the chance to thank Maurice for saving my neck, though if anything, Perry was more stunned than I was that the vampire had come to our rescue.

I snapped out of my thoughts when the door opened and Drew walked into the questioning room. "Have you finished interrogating them yet?"

"Certainly not," said Petra. "The Reaper keeps deflecting instead of answering my questions."

"It won't kill you to learn my name," I muttered, rubbing my shins under the table. I'd woken up with bruises up to my knees, not to mention an ache in my neck from ducking my head under the low tunnel ceiling. Petra, of course, had zero sympathy to speak of.

"The leader of the Wardens' team has already submitted

their report, so there's no need to keep questioning them." Drew's disapproval was like a laser beam focused on Petra, but the tired note to his voice showed he hadn't escaped unscathed from last night's events either.

According to Drew, I'd looked dead when the Wardens brought me back to the inn, and he still hadn't quite got over the shock. We'd had no time to talk after my brush with death, not when he'd been left to cobble together a story from Perry and the Wardens that would satisfy the rest of the police.

"There you have it," said Perry. "Our supervisors should be satisfied with Tam's report, and we don't have anything more to discuss. The ghouls were destroyed."

"Unless the person responsible for setting them loose in town comes back," I added. "Then we'll have another problem."

Petra lifted her head sharply. "Your report mentioned nothing about another person's involvement."

"You already *read* the report?" Perry said. "What was the point in dragging us here?"

I could guess. She'd been trying to find a way to get me into trouble, to poke holes in my story, and to otherwise ruin my day.

"To ensure our own records are complete," said Petra. "Strange… I don't recall your report having quite as detailed an account of the events in these supposed tunnels as the one you gave to me."

"What's that mean?" Perry asked.

"You claimed to be trapped underground," said Petra. "The report your team leader sent in didn't mention anything about these wards you said you found etched into the walls."

Perry squared her shoulders. "Obviously. It's not relevant. We were supposed to report on the ghouls, not the tunnels."

"Naturally, but one might think that someone was trying to avoid another visit from the Wardens' supervisors in the future." Petra watched me through narrowed eyes. "Wouldn't you say?"

Dammit. She had me there. While I hadn't helped the Wardens compile the report, I'd gathered that Drew had worked with Tam to ensure that all bases were covered and that there were no risks of another "unplanned" visit from the higher-ups. Especially if Mina Devlin tried any more trickery.

"Who *wants* a visit from the Wardens' supervisors?" Perry asked. "I wouldn't. Except for mine, of course. Kellen is cool, but otherwise, the bosses are no fun to be around."

"Is that so?" Petra said in a disinterested tone. "I was asking the Reaper."

She just wouldn't quit. "I don't mind the Wardens sending their supervisors here if they think our story is incomplete, but that would involve asking why the police didn't investigate the tunnel themselves, wouldn't it?"

Her smug expression slipped a little, and Perry gave me a sly smile.

"As it happens, I think this is worth investigating," said Drew. "Maura and Perry almost drowned. Someone intentionally trapped them underground."

"Again, you refer to a person, but you refuse to name names."

"Mina Devlin." I all but spat out the words. "Her or one of her minions. Are you happy now?"

"That," she said, "is no way to address an officer of the law."

"That's enough," Drew said in warning tones. "Maura is recovering from an ordeal. So is Perry. There's no need to keep them here any longer."

The two exchanged a mutual glare that seemed to last a

lot longer than a few seconds. Then Petra indicated the door. "The Wardens' job is done. There's no need for any further enquiries. You may leave."

Good. I guess she won't investigate the tunnels. Not that anyone would be able to get inside until the water levels were lower, and I hadn't any fortitude left for an argument with someone who'd have been happy to let me drown.

"Come on." Drew beckoned to us to leave, and I rose shakily to my feet. I hated showing weakness in front of Petra, but she was the one who'd dragged me here first thing in the morning after I'd nearly drowned. My whole body felt like one giant bruise. I clenched my teeth and did my best to walk upright, not hunched over, as I'd have preferred.

Once we were outside the room, Drew put an arm around me. "Are you okay?"

"As I'll ever be." I coughed, and he wrapped his other arm around me, drawing me into a hug.

His mouth brushed my ear. "Don't do that to me again, Maura. I thought you were dead."

Instead of reassuring him I wouldn't, I simply hugged him back and buried my head in his shoulder. "It wasn't that fun for me either."

Hearing the front door opening, I reluctantly let him go. Drew's warm hand closed around mine as he walked me to the door, through which the Wardens had just left.

"I wish I could come back with you," he said.

"You have to stop Petra from making any more phone calls to the Wardens' supervisors, right?"

"Maura." His lips pressed together. "Would it be a bad thing if the Wardens' supervisors got involved in hunting Mina Devlin?"

"No, but I doubt that's what she had in mind." Man, I was exhausted. "Since when was she in charge of deciding whether it's worth the police investigating a potential threat or not?"

"She isn't, and this tunnel's discovery might backfire in Mina's face rather than work in her favour."

"Yeah… I bet she was hiding all sorts of nefarious stuff in there." When the water levels went down, we'd have our chance to look and secure the place. Assuming she hadn't set up another booby trap to ensnare the next unfortunate soul to wander in. "For years. That's what bothers me the most. Someone was redoing the sealing spells over and over again."

"Exactly." A grim note entered his tone. "If she's planning to make a move, what we don't need is more division. Can you try to avoid getting into any more fights with my officers?"

My shoulders slumped. "All right. But if Mina sends another ghoul, I'm putting it in Petra's office."

Mina Devlin's fingerprints are all over this. Why is Petra being such an obstructionist? She was dangerous in a way that few other people were, because the authority structure in Hawkwood Hollow wasn't as rigid as it might've been in a larger community than this one. She could easily amass enough supporters to go against Drew's orders—and she'd already done so once.

Of course, I'd have made more headway if I'd managed to bring her actual proof of what lurked in the tunnels, but I didn't have any photos of the marks on the walls. Our phones hadn't survived their soaking, and Drew's frantic attempts to reach me had been for nothing.

After a last hug from Drew, I left the police station and walked straight through my brother's ghost.

"Really, Mart?" I stumbled and nearly fell over, grabbing a lamppost with one hand to steady myself. "I'm already freezing enough."

"You left me behind."

I let go of the lamppost. "Did you want to listen to Petra annoy the crap out of me for hours?"

"No, I want to see what she does when she finds out I removed every staple from her stapler and hid them around in her office."

I choked on a laugh. "When did you have time to do that?"

"Last night," he replied. "I followed her to the police station after you went back to the inn."

"You knew I was still alive, I assume."

"Obviously." He drifted alongside me as I walked away from the police station. "I'd know if you were dead."

"Yeah." *Honestly. Way to forget the obvious, Maura.* "Did *you* know we could communicate with each other like that? In our minds, I mean?"

"Well, yes," he said. "It's how you brought me back."

My mouth dropped open. "Huh?"

"You called me back from the other side," he said. "Not just with your voice but using your Reaper powers too."

My mind reeled. "But I—I couldn't use my powers in the tunnel. Someone used a more powerful version of the coven's booby trap on me."

"Well, they didn't try hard enough," he said smugly. "You bound me to you, remember? No spell can erase that."

"I couldn't reach the afterworld." My chest tightened. His words brought to my mind the sheer desperation I'd felt while in the tunnel, the waters closing in. When I'd called him back, I must have tapped into the same layer of emotion that I'd reached when he died, when I'd brought him back from the brink of true death and saved him from passing into the afterworld forever. The memory of the worst day of my life was hazy, and I'd done my best to block it out, but I'd never forgotten entirely.

I blinked, my eyes stinging. "I'm glad you were able to bring *me* back this time."

"Did you think I'd let you leave without any warning?" He surprised me with a hug—a cold, ghostly one—but this time, I didn't mind the chill. "I don't think so."

"What do I owe you?" I squinted at him suspiciously. "A lifetime of being in charge of movie night?"

"Hardly," he said. "I have an unfair advantage against most people in the 'lifetime' department."

"That's true." I resumed walking. "I'll think of something later."

When the bridge came into view, I slowed my pace, but all traces of the fight with the ghouls had vanished, washed away by the waters. My legs ached at the memory, and I let Mart overtake me.

"I have an idea." He glided to a halt at the edge, humming under his breath. "Yes… perfect."

"What's perfect?"

"As payment for my saving your life," he said, "you don't get to complain about my singing ever again."

I groaned. "Seriously?"

"Oh yeah." He grinned, and I almost forgot the surging river below the bridge as I contemplated the horror of a lifetime of listening to him sing the Pokémon theme without ever being allowed to raise a single complaint.

Behind him, I glimpsed several figures through the inn's front doors. "Hey, looks like our guests are leaving."

"Are they?" He twirled on the spot. "I shall give that vampire a reason to think twice about coming back."

"Mart, he did save my life." I quickened my pace, crossing the bridge as fast as possible with my shaky legs. "He brought you to help me, too, didn't he?"

"He's still a terrible guest." Nevertheless, he slowed to let me catch up instead of pursuing the vampire. "You're too generous. He left you in the water to drown."

"He knew you'd help me get out." I wasn't certain on that,

but we'd already been out of the tunnel at that point, and I didn't blame him for prioritising his teammate. "Can you imagine a vampire being indebted to a Reaper? I don't envy Perry for having to be nice to him from now on."

"I'm sure he'll leave a dead rat in her bed to restore normality."

"Rats. Ugh." He probably would too. "I hope he didn't leave any in his room."

"He didn't. I checked when I was hiding all his socks."

"Mart." I halted in front of the inn. "I thought you said you didn't mess with him."

"Much." He wore an angelic smile as he drifted into the lobby, and I shook my head at him.

If the vampire had left a rat in *my* bed… Well, it was a reminder that Mart's singing was far from the worst form of torment he could inflict on someone. Luckily, the vampire wasn't paying him any attention. When I walked into the lobby, I found Tam arguing with Allie over the discount she'd given them on their rooms.

"This isn't necessary," he protested. "We're more than happy to pay."

"You helped save the inn," Allie said. "We wouldn't have anything left if not for you."

"We were just doing our jobs," Callum mumbled, his face brick red.

"Exactly." Farley's pale face was flushed with embarrassment too. "It was Perry who did most of the work—and Maura, of course."

"If not for you, I'd be a goner," I said to her. "You're the one who turned off the wards trapping us in the tunnel, aren't you?"

I hadn't been fully aware at the time, but when I'd regained consciousness for a brief period after my arrival back at the inn, I'd been mildly confused to see Farley climbing out of the river. Given that she was the only witch on the team aside from Perry, she must have been responsible for undoing the spell keeping us imprisoned in the darkness.

Farley went even redder. "I'm not much good in combat. I had to do something to help."

"How'd you even get into the tunnel?" I couldn't picture the petite witch holding her breath for long enough to swim all the way to the second chamber.

"I used a water-breathing spell," she replied. "Why didn't you two do the same?"

"Didn't think," Perry said sheepishly. "You saved both our necks."

When the vampire raised an eyebrow at us, I added, "Yes, and you, too, Maurice. Does the rule about not crossing running water not apply to swimming in it?"

"We *can* cross the water," he muttered. "We just don't like it."

"Good to know." I paused, another thought occurring to me. "Ah—there *isn't* another vampire in town, is there? Was it a ghoul you saw the other night?"

"Must have been."

That made sense, but a thread of doubt remained, especially as I didn't know if Mina herself had been in the tunnels or someone else had been responsible for trapping us.

Tam stepped back from the front desk. "I've left my number in case you need to reach me again. Like I said, the Wardens covered all our expenses, so I left a tip."

It was Allie's turn to flush. "Really, it's unnecessary."

"We won't trouble you any longer," added Callum. "Shall we be off?"

"Yes." The vampire didn't offer anyone a goodbye, leaving the inn ahead of the others. Farley went next, followed by Callum and Tam.

Perry slowed to let me catch up to her outside. "Let me know if you need my help at any point in the future. I'd leave my contact number, but my phone…"

"Mine's in the same state." Even magic hadn't been able to save my mobile phone from its unfortunate soaking. "I'll work something out. You said you had a decent supervisor?"

"Tam left the office's number with the police—with Drew," she told me. "If you need us, just call and ask for Kellen."

"Good," I said. "I'll ask him to see if we can put some of your people on the task of hunting down our missing coven leader too."

"Wise idea," she said. "Ah—you should know that Tam asked who initially got the call to the Wardens' office, offering the mission. They said it was a female officer from Hawkwood Hollow."

Petra. "Yeah, I figured. I'll handle her."

"If you're sure." When her team waved her over, she gave me a final smile. "See you around."

I raised my hand in farewell, my mind already churning over the possibilities of Petra's reasoning for contacting the Wardens' office. How much had she known about the true nature of the disappearances? Had she just been trying to get me into trouble, or was there another, even more sinister motive?

Later. Think about that later.

When I walked back into the inn, Carey came running over and hugged me. "Maura, are you okay?"

"Sure." I hitched on a smile. "Might need to take another nap, but I'm good."

"You were lucky." Allie came out from the desk and hugged me too. "You're still freezing cold."

"A movie night wrapped up in blankets will solve that," I

said. "Relax, I'm fine. The Wardens left because the ghouls have gone. We're safe."

"I hope we *don't* need their help again," Carey remarked. "Is the tunnel... Is the tunnel still there?"

"It's flooded," I replied. "Nobody can get in."

Until the water levels lowered... and given the sound of rain splashing on the ground outside, that might be a while yet. Fine by me. I needed to recuperate, and then I'd make a plan.

If another flood was coming, I would need to be ready for it.

ABOUT THE AUTHOR

Elle Adams lives in the middle of England, where she spends most of her time reading an ever-growing mountain of books, planning her next adventure, or writing. Elle's books are humorous mysteries with a paranormal twist, packed with magical mayhem.

She also writes urban and contemporary fantasy novels as Emma L. Adams.

Find out more about Elle's books at: https://www. elleadamsauthor.com/

Find Elle on Facebook at https://www.facebook. com/pg/ElleAdamsAuthor/